SANDRA WOLFF • JARED BAREL

DARK CLOUD

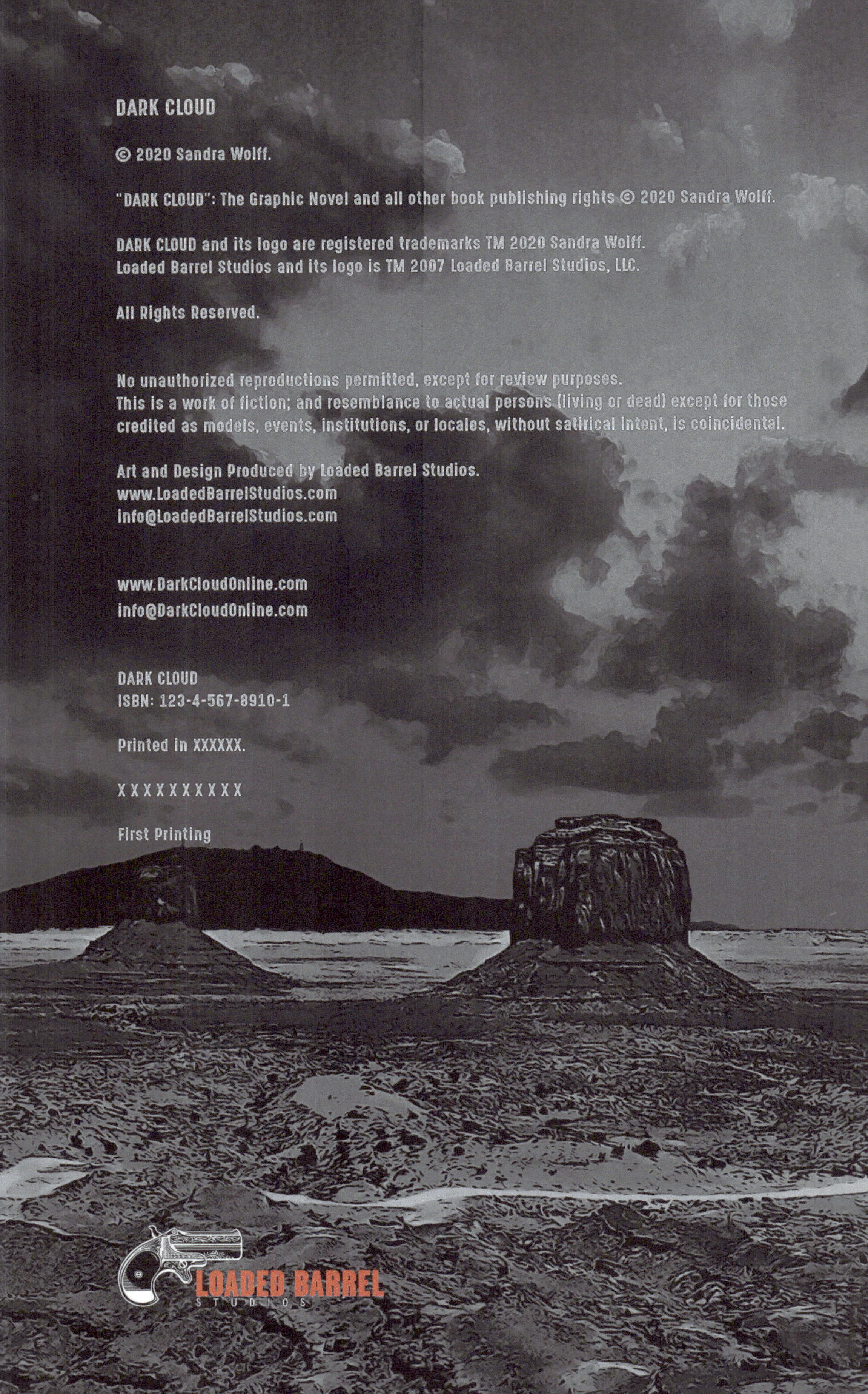

Loaded Barrel
STUDIOS

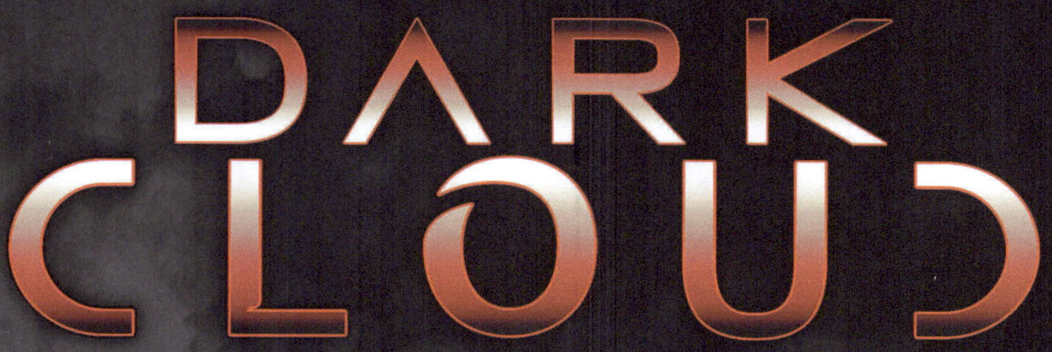

DARK CLOUD

CREATED BY
SANDRA WOLFF

WRITTEN BY
JARED BAREL

BASED ON THE SCREENPLAY BY
SANDRA WOLFF

ART BY
JARED BAREL

LETTERING AND BOOK DESIGN BY
JARED BAREL

ART AND DESIGN PRODUCED BY
LOADED BARREL STUDIOS

FOREWORD

I created DARK CLOUD out of my own experiences. This all started when I fell in love with the George Miller film THE ROAD WARRIOR. What could top that? Then I started to think further. Why were we looking to Australia for a desert? We've got a wonderful Wild West here. Granted, it's hard to get even 100 miles away from a gas station, which is a bummer, but it's here. And why did the main character have to be male? Technology is a great equalizer, and I used to be pretty kick-butt myself. The skills that the main character in this story has are skills that I also have. We're only talking a matter of degree, though I'm definitely no action hero in real life. Never was.

But there's more to it than that. A lot of people liked THE ROAD WARRIOR, so why me? Actually, that movie only gave this project the basic idea, but it wasn't the drive. (Sorry George, but at least I mention you first.)

I also created DARK CLOUD out of my own frustrations. I was just out of college with a theoretical degree, and the rug yanked out from under my career plans - again (don't ask). No job skills. No real world skills. I didn't even know how to type. I felt like I had been sold a bill of goods. "Get a degree, any degree, and you'll get a great job." That stopped being true back in the 1950's. But there I was, theoretically 'educated,' unable to go on for the graduate degree I knew I needed - and wanted, and feeling very frustrated. I began to go through my own 'Angry Young Woman' phase.

It burned in me, and the alter ego of Dark Cloud surfaced and made herself known. I began to think, "I can't be the only one." There had to be other young women out there, 'educated' or not, who burned with that frustrated knowledge that they were more than just grunt laborers, drab, non-descript, required by society to be 'nice and sweet,' frilly, and cute if they wanted a job (I noticed that my male counter-parts were getting away with attitude a lot more than I was, which rubbed me to no end), - and had that fiery vibrance inside them, capable of so much more than the role a perceived 'system' would have them fill.

I decided to share what had emerged in me with the world. Hey, I didn't have anything else going on after my latest choice of careers paths got blocked (after years of study - talk about frustrating!) "Screw it," I said. "I'm going to set the most outrageous goal possible. I'm going to make a really good feature-length film that gets cinematic distribution. Let's see how far I get..."

To do that I needed a story. I began developing a story. To tell it, I had to present it in a format people would accept. I began learning how to write a screenplay.

Then something interesting happened...

I began to learn real world skills. First, I had to learn how to type and be organized. I went back to school and learned administrative assistant skills. I learned business organization and how to present myself. Then I finished my first draft of the screenplay. It was BAD. "Rewrite Needed," doesn't begin to describe it. So I started working on a rewrite.

But I looked at the script and asked myself, "How does a movie get made from here?" (I still want a movie out of this.) "Oh! It's somewhat like putting together a small business." I started reading books on business and taking classes in that direction.

Something interesting began happening again...

I realized that I was beginning to figure out how society itself works, as though the pieces of a giant jig-saw puzzle were falling into place. I don't have that puzzle completely solved yet, but I've got some good sections.

Even the way I was thinking began to change...

The journey has been continuing ever since. It hasn't been a straight line. That's for sure. But it has moved forward.

Fear not! The young woman who starts out as Dark Cloud can become Cleopatra VII in her own right further down the road. That Cleopatra still has Dark Cloud in her, and keeps the leather jacket in the back of her closet, ready to bring out should the day ever return when she has to go kick butt in person again, but she never would have become that powerful, effective woman were it not for the 'bad girl' of Dark Cloud.

I really feel those young women who get labeled 'bad girls' are being seen through the wrong light. They have the potential to become Cleopatras. Hey! Did that Egyptian Queen ever have to act like Tourist Guide Barbie just so she'd keep her job as a receptionist? And what's this bull that if she doesn't pull that off successfully, then she can't do bigger and better things instead? I do get mad at those social messages. They're real, too. They need to go.

These are the heroes we need. From Dark Cloud to Cleopatra, it's all on the same continuum.

I'm still working on Cleopatra. When I control more real estate than the modern day country of Egypt, and have life and death say over millions, I'll let you know. Then I can stop reaching higher and further, becoming yet more, refusing to let someone else define me.

-Sandra

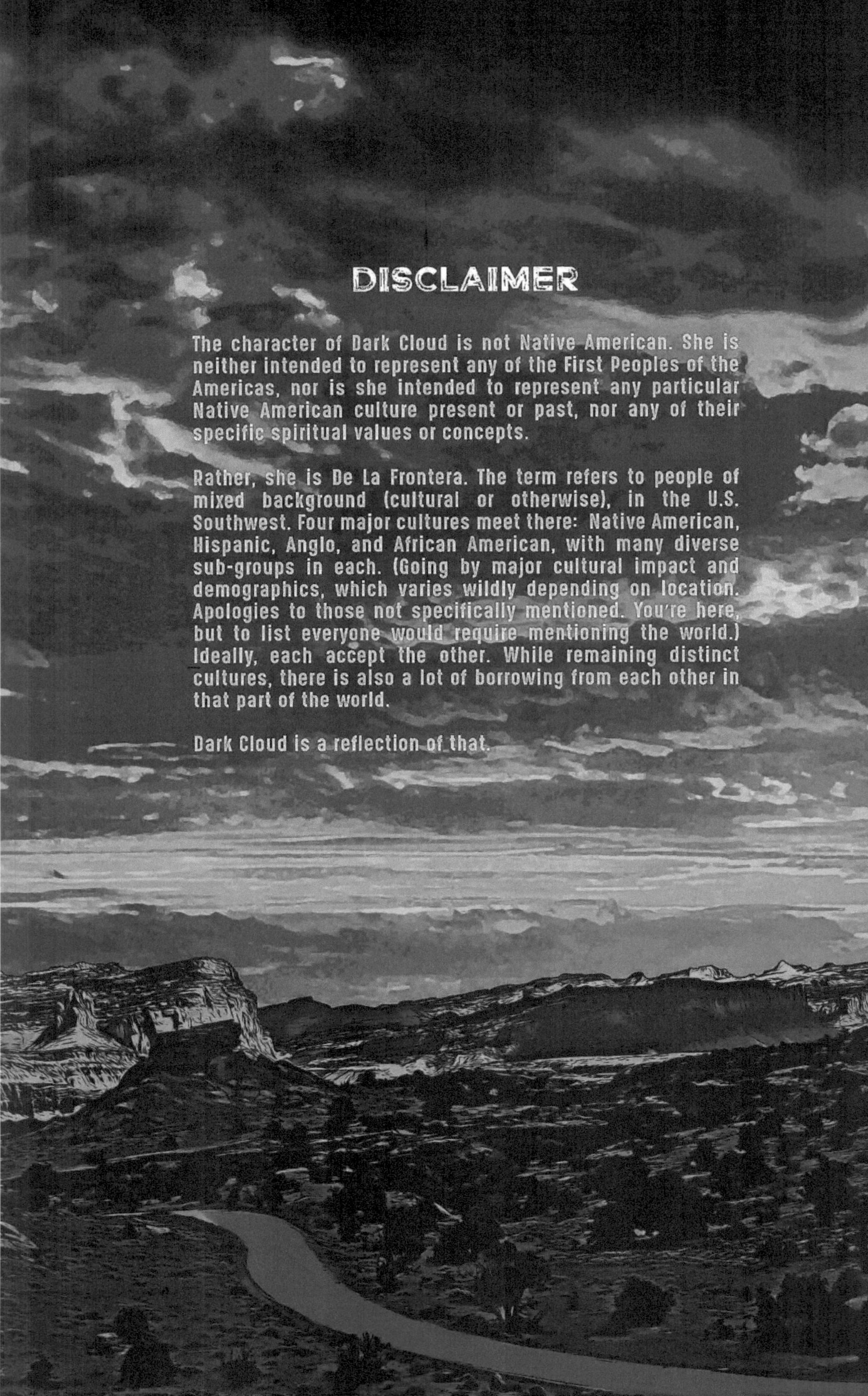

DISCLAIMER

The character of Dark Cloud is not Native American. She is neither intended to represent any of the First Peoples of the Americas, nor is she intended to represent any particular Native American culture present or past, nor any of their specific spiritual values or concepts.

Rather, she is De La Frontera. The term refers to people of mixed background (cultural or otherwise), in the U.S. Southwest. Four major cultures meet there: Native American, Hispanic, Anglo, and African American, with many diverse sub-groups in each. (Going by major cultural impact and demographics, which varies wildly depending on location. Apologies to those not specifically mentioned. You're here, but to list everyone would require mentioning the world.) Ideally, each accept the other. While remaining distinct cultures, there is also a lot of borrowing from each other in that part of the world.

Dark Cloud is a reflection of that.

CHAPTER 1

THE LAND...

...MY HOME.

FROM WHAT I'M TOLD, LAND IN THIS TERRITORY ISN'T ALL THAT DIFFERENT FROM WHAT IT WAS BEFORE.
WE'RE LUCKY IN THAT ASPECT.
THE PEOPLE, ON THE OTHER HAND...
...I DON'T KNOW IF THE SAME CAN BE SAID ABOUT THEM.
IT'S A DIFFERENT WORLD SINCE IT HAPPENED. SOCIETY TODAY IS PRIMITIVE. FEUDAL. YOU HAVE TO FIGHT FOR WHAT YOU HAVE...
...TO KEEP WHAT YOU HAVE.
MONEY MEANS NOTHING. THERE'S NO ONE TO CASH YOUR BITCOINS OR WHATEVER. WE LIVE OFF THE LAND. TRADE WITH OUR NEIGHBORS. FOOD. RESOURCES.
WE GET BY.

IT WASN'T THE SAME FOR EVERYONE.

THE PEOPLE THAT USED TO WORK IN TALL BUILDINGS AND DRIVE SHINY CARS LOST EVERYTHING WHEN IT ALL CAME CRASHING DOWN.

A SCARED ANIMAL WILL LASH OUT IF IT THINKS ITS LIFE DEPENDS ON IT. PEOPLE ARE NO DIFFERENT.

WHEN THE FIRST OF THE WARLORDS CAME TO POWER, WE THOUGHT IT WAS JUST A PROBLEM FOR THE LARGER CITIES IN THE COASTAL TERRITORIES.

WE WERE WRONG.

THERE'S A WAR RAGING FOR CONTROL OF THE LAND.

THIS LAND IS MINE... WELL, OURS... ALL OF OURS... IT'S ALL WE HAVE. AND I WILL FIGHT TO PROTECT IT.

WELCOME TO THE FUTURE WEST.

I LOVE THIS LAND. IT LIVES AND BREATHES; ENGULFING AND EMBRACING. THE LAND GIVES WITHOUT TAKING.
IT'S HOW OUR ANCESTORS SURVIVED AND IT'S HOW WE'LL SURVIVE.

THE LAND SPEAKS TO ME. SHE SHOWS ME A DIFFERENT VIEW OF THE WORLD. IT'S LIKE EXPERIENCING THE VIBRATION OF A CRYSTAL POWERING A QUARTZ WATCH.
CALL IT A SIXTH SENSE. A GIFT. I DUNNO. MAYBE I'M JUST THE ONLY ONE PAYING ATTENTION WHEN SHE SPEAKS.

BLAM
THIS DEER GIVES ITS LIFE SO THAT MY FAMILY CAN EAT.
I THANK HER.

WHAT THE--?

HEY! YOU! DON'T MOVE!
OH, SHIT. MERCENARIES. SOLDIERS FOR THE LOCAL WARLORD.

THESE GUYS AREN'T THE PRISONER TAKING TYPE... NOT THAT I'D LET MYSELF BE TAKEN PRISONER.
I KNOW THIS TERRAIN BETTER THAN HIM. I'LL LOSE HIM AND CIRCLE BACK FOR THE DEER.
IT BETTER NOT SPOIL.

SHIT. I SHOULDN'T HAVE BEEN WORRIED ABOUT THE DEER.
A SECOND MERC. I DIDN'T SEE HIM.

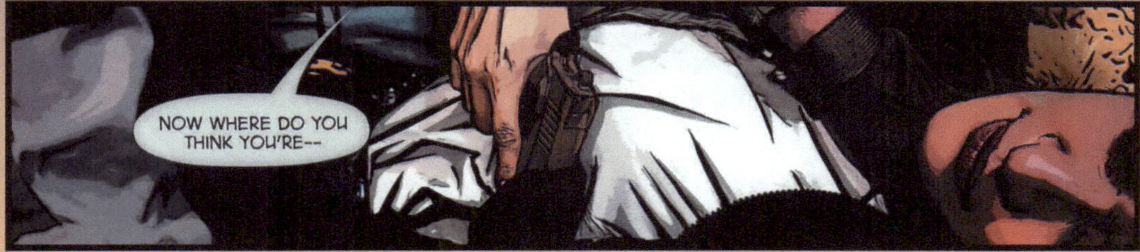

NOW WHERE DO YOU THINK YOU'RE--

DAMMIT! I HATE TO WASTE THE BULLET, I'M RUNNING LOW...
BANG

...BUT THAT SEEMED LIKE A WORTHY CAUSE.

SUDDENLY, I CAN'T BREATHE.
THE WEIGHT OF THE BOLA SWINGS AROUND MY THROAT. I ONLY HAVE A FEW SECONDS.
YOU'RE A FEISTY ONE. COULD IT BE THAT ALL THE TROUBLE THAT'S BEEN COMIN' OUTTA THIS SECTOR IS FROM YOU?
NAH. LOOKS LIKE YOU'RE NOT SO TOUGH AFTER ALL.
DO SOMETHING. ANYTHING. LIGHTS ARE GOING DARK.
AAHHH!!!
BITCH!
SLAP!
AAAHHH!!!

PLEASE!!!
PLEASE!!!
THAT WAS GRAPHIC.
WHAT TOOK YOU SO LONG? A COUPLE MORE SECONDS AND RICARDO WOULD BE HAVING VENISON WITHOUT ME.
I CAN BREATHE AGAIN. I COULD'VE TAKEN THAT GUY, I MEAN... I SHOULD'VE TAKEN THAT GUY. THANK THE FORCES OF EARTH AND SKY FOR KLAATH.
COUGH *COUGH*
MY APOLOGIES. I MISJUDGED THE PROBABILITY OF YOUR SURVIVAL FOR 10 MINUTES WITHOUT ME.
OKAY, WELL, THAT'S JUST MEAN... THERE WERE TWO OF THEM! I GOT THE FIRST GUY.
AS I SAID. I MISJUDGED.
HE'S NOT MUCH FOR CONVERSATION, BUT I KNOW HE'LL NEVER FAIL HIS PROTOCOL TO KEEP ME ALIVE.
THERE IS A CONVOY EN ROUTE...
...I WILL DISPOSE OF THE BODIES ACCORDINGLY.
CAN'T SAY THE SAME FOR ANYONE WHO ATTEMPTS TO CHALLENGE THAT PROTOCOL.

THOSE MEN WERE A SYMPTOM OF AN EVER-INCREASING PRESENCE OF THE LOCAL WARLORD'S REACH OVER THIS TERRITORY.

THE NEW ECONOMY IS A BARTER SYSTEM. NOT JUST BETWEEN PEOPLE OR VILLAGES, BUT BETWEEN TERRITORIES. BETWEEN THE WARLORDS.
HOW LONG UNTIL THEY MAKE IT BACK TO THEIR COMPOUND?

THE SIZE OF THE CARAVAN REQUIRES A LONGER ROUTE THROUGH THE RAVINE. THEY SHOULD ARRIVE BY DAYBREAK TOMORROW.
THE WARLORDS THAT CONTROL THE COASTS ARE IN CONTROL OF THE PORTS AND HAVE COMMAND OF OVERSEAS TRADE.

I NEED AMMO. I'M RUNNING LOW. I SHOULDN'T BE DEBATING WHETHER OR NOT TO SHOOT SOMEONE TRYING TO KILL ME BECAUSE I'M TRYING TO SAVE BULLETS. WE SHOULD MAKE A RUN TONIGHT BEFORE THEY MAKE THEIR ARRIVAL.
THE WARLORDS IN THE LANDLOCKED TERRITORIES ACQUIRE RESOURCES TO BARTER WITH THE COASTAL TERRITORIES FOR ITEMS WE DON'T GET THIS FAR INLAND. MANUFACTURED GOODS. PROCESSED FOODS... MUNITIONS – WHICH THE WARLORD DOESN'T SHARE.

I HATE THIS PART OF THE TRIP. EVERYONE KNOWS THERE ARE EVIL SPIRITS IN THIS SECTOR. IT'S HAUNTED.

HAUNTED?! FERCHRISSAKES, PULL YOUR SHIT TOGETHER, CORPORAL.

THE LOCAL WARLORD, HE CALLS HIMSELF GENERAL STONE, IS A SLAVE DRIVER – WELL, THEY'RE NOT SLAVES EXACTLY, BUT THEY MIGHT AS WELL BE – HE HAS THEM MINING FOR ORE ALL ACROSS THE TERRITORY. THE MINES SEEM TO BE POPPING UP MORE AND MORE LATELY.

I REFUSE TO LET HIM EXPAND HIS MINING EXPEDITION INTO OUR HOMELAND.

THUD!

KLAATU AND I HAVE TAKEN IT UPON OURSELVES TO KEEP HIM OUT.

KLAATU DISPOSES OF THE MERCENARIES' BODIES.

I TOLD YOU! EVIL SPIRITS!

THIS IS OUR LAND.

WE SHOULDN'T BE HERE!
IF YOU'RE GOING TO CONTINUE TO BE INSUBORDINATE AT LEAST DO IT WITH A SHRED OF SELF-RESPECT. YOU'RE A SOLDIER GODDAMMIT.

GENERAL STONE? SOMETHING BIG MUST BE GOING ON. HE DOESN'T USUALLY GO OUT ON THESE CONVOYS PERSONALLY.
YOU SEEING ANYTHING I'M NOT SEEING?
YES.

I'LL SHOW YOU EVIL SPIRITS.

BOOM!

IT'S TIME TO GO.

THE DEER WILL KEEP US FED FOR A LITTLE WHILE. THE HIDE WILL BE GOOD FOR TRADING.
RICARDO SAYS I WAS BORN FOR THIS WORLD. HE SAYS I WOULD HAVE BEEN LOST IN THE OLD WORLD.
I DON'T REMEMBER MUCH OF THE OLD WORLD. MY MEMORY OF EVERYTHING BEFORE RICARDO FOUND ME IS HAZY, LIKE A DREAM... OR A NIGHTMARE. IMAGES FLOATING IN THE ETHER.
THOSE MEMORIES DON'T FEEL REAL ANYMORE.
IT DOESN'T MATTER. THIS IS REALITY NOW. THIS WORLD. SURVIVAL. THIS IS WHAT'S REAL.
RICARDO SAYS THAT'S PROBABLY WHY I'VE ADAPTED SO WELL TO THIS WORLD. I'M THE ONLY ONE NOT HOLDING ON TO A PAST I'LL NEVER GET BACK.
HE SAYS HE HOPES I REMEMBER ONE DAY, BUT IT HAS TO BE ON MY OWN TERMS. I'M NOT SURE WHAT HE MEANS. MAYBE I'LL FIND OUT IF THAT DAY EVER COMES.
MAYBE I'M BETTER OFF NOT REMEMBERING. I CAN'T IMAGINE ANYTHING GOOD HAPPENED TO LEAD ME TO STARVING HALF TO DEATH IN THE MIDDLE OF THE DESERT.

<RICARDO! WE'RE HOME AND WE HAVE DINNER!...WELL, IT'LL BE DINNER.>
RICARDO AND I COMMUNICATE IN SPANISH, HIS NATIVE TONGUE. RICARDO DE CASTILE.
HE'S NOT GOING TO BE HAPPY. I WON'T BE ABLE TO HIDE THAT I WAS IN A FIGHT.
DARK CLOUD, WELCOME HOME, MY CHILD. YOUR NECK! WHAT HAPPENED?
IT'S NOTHING. I'M FINE. I HANDLED IT... KLAATU HELPED.
COME, KLAATU. WE'LL SEE JUST HOW FINE SHE IS.
RICARDO WEARS THE ROBES OF A FRANCISCAN MONK TO HIDE HIS IDENTITY. HE WAS A SCIENTIST IN THE OLD WORLD. AN ENGINEER. BUT TO ME, HE'S A WIZARD.
SATISFIED?
HE BUILT KLAATU. A RELIC OF A WORLD WHOSE TECHNOLOGY WAS ITS GREATEST ACHIEVEMENT AND ITS TRAGIC DOWNFALL.
WHEN HE FOUND ME, HE REPROGRAMMED THE COMBAT ROBOT TO BE MY PROTECTOR AND PUT A CHIP IN MY FOREARM SO HE COULD ALWAYS FIND ME.
I NAMED HIM KLAATU AFTER A CHARACTER IN AN OLD FILM I REMEMBER SEEING AS A CHILD. IT'S FUNNY THE THINGS YOU REMEMBER AND THE THINGS YOU DON'T.
YOU HAVE A UNIQUE ABILITY TO SEE THE UNSEEN, MARIPOSA. BUT YOU ARE NOT INVINCIBLE. THESE ARE DANGEROUS TIMES AND THE LAND IS FILLED WITH DANGEROUS MEN.
WE NEEDED THE MEAT.
THE MERCENARIES ARE MOVING DEEPER INTO OUR TERRITORY. I THINK THEY'RE SCOUTING TO EXPAND THEIR MINING OPERATION. IF THEY EXPAND OVER THE MESA WE WON'T BE ABLE TO HOLD THEM OFF. WE EITHER FIGHT FOR OUR LAND NOW OR END UP SLAVES LIKE THE OTHERS.
YOUR LIFE IS TOO HIGH A PRICE TO PAY FOR OUR FREEDOM. I CANNOT LOSE YOU, MARIPOSA.
I WANT TO ASSURE HIM THAT HE WON'T, BUT TODAY WAS A CLOSE CALL. I HAVE TO BE STRONGER.

I HAVE TO TELL YOU SOMETHING.
RICARDO HAS NEVER SHOWN ME ANYTHING BUT KINDNESS.
HE DIDN'T HAVE TO TAKE ME IN. TO CARE FOR ME. TO LOVE ME.

GENERAL STONE WAS IN THE CONVOY MAKING ITS WAY THROUGH THE RAVINE. I'M LOW ON AMMO. WE NEED TRIGGERS AND POWDER. KLAATU AND I ARE GOING TO GO STOCK UP AT THE MUNITIONS DUMP AT THE COMPOUND. I'M GOING TO TRY AND FIND OUT WHAT STONE'S UP TO.
I THINK IT BREAKS HIS HEART THAT I CAN'T ALLOW MYSELF TO JUST STAY HERE AND TEND TO THE CROPS AND THE CHICKENS.

YOU KNOW HOW I FEEL ABOUT YOU RAIDING STONE'S COMPOUND.
WE'VE DONE THIS RUN COUNTLESS TIMES. THE BUNKER IS POORLY GUARDED AND THEY STILL HAVEN'T LEARNED THAT THE EMERGENCY HATCH IS UNLOCKED AND UNSECURED. I ONLY TAKE WHAT I NEED AND NEVER ENOUGH FOR ANYONE TO TAKE ANY REAL NOTICE.
I KNOW HE SEES ME AS WILD, FERAL. AND YET HIS LOVE FOR ME NEVER WAIVERS.

DARK CLOUD, GENERAL STONE IS NOT SOMEONE TO PLAY GAMES WITH. I KNEW HIM ONCE UPON A TIME WHEN I WORKED FOR THE GOVERNMENT... WHEN THERE STILL WAS A GOVERNMENT. HE'S A DANGEROUS MAN.
HE'S THE FATHER I SHOULD HAVE HAD IN THE FIRST PLACE.
I FIGHT FOR OUR LAND, OUR HOME, BECAUSE I LOVE HIM AS MUCH AS I LOVE MY OWN FREEDOM.

I UNDERSTAND HIS FEARS.

BUT I CAN'T HELP BUT FEEL THERE'S DANGER BREWING ON THE HORIZON.

I'VE ALWAYS HAD A SINKING FEELING IN MY GUT THAT SOMETHING'S WRONG. THAT FEELING GROWS WITH EVERY PASSING DAY. SOMETHING IS HAPPENING INSIDE OF ME... AND AROUND ME.

I TRY TO KEEP A GRIP ON IT, BUT IT'S SLIPPING. SOMETHING HAPPENED TO ME. THERE MUST BE A DAMN GOOD REASON THAT I CAN'T REMEMBER MY OWN NAME... I WASN'T BORN *DARK CLOUD*.

I SHOULD KNOW BETTER THAN TO GO POKING AROUND FOR ANSWERS.

BUT LATELY, I CAN'T SHAKE THE FEELING THAT SOMETHING MAY BE LOOMING OVER THE FUTURE.

MAYBE RICARDO IS RIGHT. MAYBE I'M IN OVER MY HEAD.

<ALANTA ANANAKA.>
THE PEYOTE AIDS IN THE VISION. LOOSENS THE CONSCIOUS MIND TO WIDEN THE PERCEPTION OF THE UNCONSCIOUS.
<TS'U'UPU-I'S-MEHEN, YAKUNAH.>
WHAT IS IT YOU SEEK, DAUGHTER OF THE LAND?
THE LORD OF STORMS. ONE OF THE MANY FORCES OF THE EARTH AND SKY. AN ENTITY OF CHAOS, DESTRUCTION... THUNDERSTORMS, THINGS LIKE THAT. IT'S INTERESTING WHO AND WHAT YOU BECOME AWARE OF WITH SENSES LIKE MINE.
I LOOK TOWARD THE DIRECTION OF MY ENEMY AND SEE A GLOW. A VIBRATING OMEN. THINGS HAVE BEEN BAD, BUT I FEAR THERE IS A NEW THREAT ON THE HORIZON.
RICARDO SAYS THOSE SENSES ARE AN AUGMENTED FORM OF SYNESTHESIA... I HATE THE TERM PSYCHIC.
THE LORD OF STORMS CAN BE A GUIDE, A SAGE.
I NEED MORE INFORMATION.
YOUR FEELINGS DO NOT FAIL YOU. SOMETHING IS COMING.

WHAT AM I SUPPOSED TO DO?
EVERYTHING THAT SHOULD COME TO FRUITION WILL. ALL THAT IS MEANT TO BE SHALL BE.
I DON'T UNDERSTAND. I NEED HELP.
I AM ALONE AND THE ENEMY GROWS LARGER BY THE DAY I'M... AFRAID.
YOU ARE NOT ALONE, CHILD. WE, THE SPIRITS OF THE LAND, ARE ALWAYS WITH YOU. THE PATH LAID OUT BEFORE YOU IS YOURS AND YOURS ALONE.
THE LORD OF STORMS' WORDS FAIL TO CLEAR ANYTHING UP. I CAN'T HELP BUT FEEL MORE ALONE THAN EVER.

THE MINES.

UNDER STONE'S CONTROL, THE MEN ARE FORCED INTO MILITARISTIC ROLES. SOME GO WILLINGLY. TRIGGER HAPPY CRETONS HAPPY TO BE HANDED A RIFLE IN A LAWLESS LAND. SOME ARE THREATENED WITH HARM TO THEIR LOVED ONES.
THE WOMEN ARE FORCED TO WORK THE MINES. YOU CAN TELL WHICH ONES HAVE BEEN HERE THE LONGEST FROM THE NERVE DAMAGE THEY SUFFER WORKING WITH THE NOXIOUS CHEMICALS USED IN THE SEPARATION PROCESS.

IF IT WEREN'T FOR RICARDO, I'D PROBABLY BE WORKING A MINE JUST LIKE THIS. I'M ONE OF THE LUCKY ONES.
LET'S MOVE.

WE DO THIS RUN AS NEEDED.
THE DUMP ISN'T GUARDED. THERE'S ONLY EVER ANYONE IN THERE IF THEY'RE LOADING UP FOR A SIEGE.

CLEAR.
IT'S FAIRLY SIMPLE. THERE'S A HATCH ON THE ROOF OF THE MUNITIONS DUMP. IT'S NEVER LOCKED.
I CAN SENSE THAT NO ONE IS HERE, BUT STILL I CAREFULLY SCAN THE ROOM BEFORE DROPPING IN. I NEED TO LEARN TO TRUST MY INSTINCTS MORE..., MY SENSES MORE.
ONE TIME, KLAATU AND I PICKED THE WRONG TIME TO MAKE A PICK UP AND WOUND UP PINNED DOWN OUTSIDE THE BUNKER WAITING FOR A BATTALION TO PREP FOR A SKIRMISH WITH A NEIGHBORING WARLORD...

...WAITED ALL NIGHT TO GET A COUPLE MAGAZINES AND HALF A KILO OF POWDER.
IT'S EMPTY TONIGHT.
LET'S MAKE IT FAST. GET WHAT WE NEED AND THEN FIND OUT WHAT STONE'S UP TO.
WE TAKE WHAT WE NEED. NEVER ENOUGH FOR ANYONE TO GET SUSPICIOUS. NOT A BULLET MORE.

THE CONVOY.
STONE.

QUITE THE FANFARE FOR A RETURNING GENERAL. WAS THERE A BATTLE WE DIDN'T HEAR ABOUT?

IS THAT WHAT I THINK IT IS?

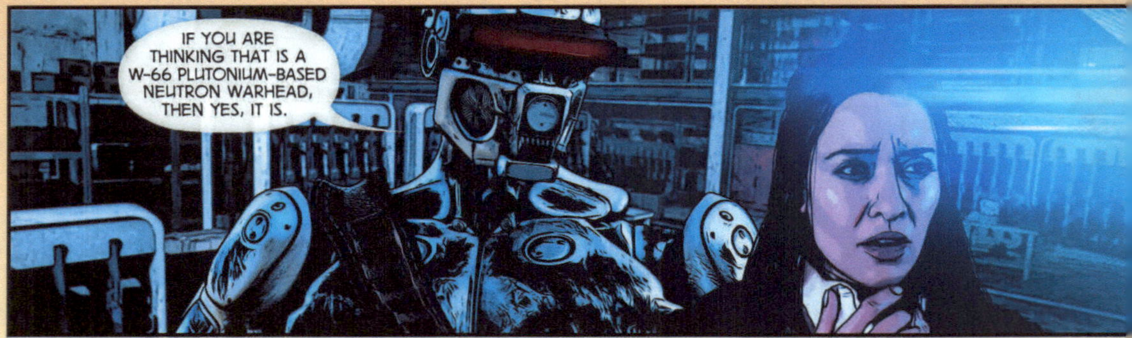

IF YOU ARE THINKING THAT IS A W-66 PLUTONIUM-BASED NEUTRON WARHEAD, THEN YES, IT IS.

A NUCLEAR BOMB! WHAT THE HELL IS STONE DOING WITH A NUKE?!

KLAATU, HACK INTO THE MAINFRAME AND SEE IF YOU CAN FIND ANYTHING. WE HAVE TO KNOW WHAT STONE IS PLANNING TO USE THAT BOMB FOR.

SIR, IT SEEMS A DIGITAL TRIPWIRE HAS BEEN TRIGGERED ON THE MAINFRAME STEMMING FROM THE MUNITIONS BUNKER. THAT COMPUTER'S ALWAYS ON THE FRITS. PROBABLY JUST A GLITCH BUT I'D LIKE TO GO CHECK IT OUT.

SOMETHING'S NOT RIGHT. WHATEVER WAS MAKING STONE HAPPY BEFORE...

...IS MAKING HIM PRETTY ANGRY NOW.
YOU SORRY EXCUSES FOR SOLDIERS!

NOT ONE MOVE.
THIS WASN'T PART OF THE PLAN.

CHAPTER 2

I SHOULDN'T HAVE LET MY GUARD DOWN...

...I COMMANDED KLAATU TO LOGIN TO THE OUTPOST'S MAINFRAME RENDERING HIM JUST LESS EFFECTIVE ENOUGH AS A GUARD DOG TO LET THIS NEANDERTHAL GET THE DROP ON US.

EVEN WITH A BARREL OF A GUN TRAINED ON ME IT'S HARD TO BE NERVOUS.

BEFORE THIS CLOWN'S SHORT STRING OF MONOSYLLABIC MACHISMO MADE IT COMPLETELY PAST HIS LIPS, KLAATU'S PROCESSOR HAD ALREADY CALCULATED THE MOST EFFICIENT METHOD OF ENDING HIS LIFE WHILE FACTORING IN THE SPEED REQUIRED TO MAKE THE KILL BEFORE I'M HARMED.

HE'S EYEING UP THE FRUITS OF OUR PILLAGE...

...NO MATTER. IN A FEW SECONDS, THIS WILL ALL BE OVER.

THE MERCENARY LOWERS HIS GUN BUT KLAATU IS ALREADY ON THE MOVE.
GO. GET OUT OF HERE.
SHIT... DID HE SAY "GET OUT OF HERE?"
KLAATU! NO! STOP!
TAKE WHAT YOU CAME FOR AND LEAVE.
HALF A SECOND LATER AND THAT GUY WOULD HAVE BEEN PULVERIZED.
I DON'T USUALLY MIND WASTING THESE PRICKS, BUT I WOULDN'T FEEL RIGHT ABOUT KILLING HIM IF HE HAD NO INTENTION OF HARMING US.
FALSE ALARM HERE. JUST ANOTHER SYSTEM GLITCH.
THANK YOU.
WHY WOULD HE LET US GO? WE DON'T STOP TO ASK. FEELS LIKE A WIN/WIN FOR EVERYONE. WE'VE GOT MORE IMPORTANT THINGS TO DEAL WITH AT THE MOMENT.

I DON'T LIKE THE LOOKS OF THAT. A LOT MORE COMMOTION THAN USUAL.

SOME KIND OF... IS THAT A BOMB? WHAT ARE YOU UP TO, STONE?

SNAP

THOUGHT YOU COULD CATCH ME OFF GUARD?!

YOU'RE NOT GONNA SHOOT ME, COYOTE JOE.
NOT THIS TIME, BLADE.
STONE SEEMS TO HAVE FOUND HIMSELF A NEW TOY. I CAN'T QUITE MAKE IT OUT. YOU HAVE ANY INTEL FOR ME?
I'VE GOT GOOD NEWS AND BAD NEWS, JOE. THE GOOD NEWS IS FINDING INTEL ON HIS "NEW TOY" WASN'T THAT DIFFICULT. HE'S PRETTY HAPPY WITH HIMSELF AND HIS LATEST ACQUISITION AND DOESN'T MIND ADVERTISING IT. THE BAD NEWS IS THAT TOY IS A NUCLEAR WARHEAD.
A NUKE! WELL THAT'S PRETTY MUCH THE WORST THING THAT COULD HAVE COME OUT OF YOUR MOUTH. WHAT'S HE DOING WITH A NUKE?
NOT SO SURE OF THE GAME PLAN, BUT RUMOR IS THE INTENDED TARGET IS THE HOOVER DAM.
THE HOOVER DAM? WHY WOULD HE BLOW UP THE HOOVER DAM? IF THAT'S GONE, THE LAND DOWNSTREAM WOULD BE PRETTY MUCH UNUSABLE BECAUSE OF THE INCREDIBLE SPRING FLOODS THAT WOULD HAPPEN ABOUT EVERY 10 YEARS.
YOUR GUESS IS AS GOOD AS MINE.
THE RESISTANCE IS ALIVE, JOE. OUR NUMBERS ARE GROWING. WE CAN PUT A STOP TO STONE AND FREE THESE PEOPLE.
I APPRECIATE THE OPTIMISM.
WE'RE NOT ALONE. JUST TONIGHT I MET A COUPLE REBELS STEALING FROM THE MUNITIONS DUMP... AND HERE I THOUGHT YOU WERE THE ONE STEALING MORE THAN I KNEW HOW TO COVER FOR. TURNS OUT WE'RE NOT THE ONLY ONES USING STONE'S WEAPONS AGAINST HIM.
GREAT, NOW ALL WE HAVE TO DO IS STOP HIM FROM NUKING THE HOOVER DAM.

IT'S HARD NOT TO IMAGINE THE WORST.
AS IF THIS PLANET HASN'T SEEN ENOUGH DESTRUCTION.
A RECKLESS MEGALOMANIAC WARLORD IS GOING TO TEAR AWAY AT WHAT'S LEFT OF IT.
WE COULD HAVE BUILT UTOPIA, INSTEAD MAN BUILT THE BOMB.

PEOPLE DON'T DESERVE THE LAND THEY WERE BORN ON.
MAYBE THAT'S WHY THE LORD OF STORMS SAID WHATEVER IS MEANT TO BE WILL BE...
...MAYBE, BUT THAT DOESN'T MEAN I'M GOING TO SIT IDLY BY AND WATCH IT BURN.

A NUCLEAR BOMB... STONE'S GOT A GODDAM NUKE.
KLAATU! PLAYBACK.
KLAATU SAID IT'S A... A... A W-66 PLUTONIUM...
A W-66 PLUTONIUM-BASED NEUTRON WARHEAD. AN ENHANCED RADIATION WEAPON.
WHAT DOES THAT MEAN?
IT'S A LOW YIELD THERMONUCLEAR WEAPON DESIGNED TO MAXIMIZE LETHAL NEUTRON RADIATION WHILE MINIMIZING THE PHYSICAL BLAST. IT WAS ORIGINALLY DESIGNED TO BE A SHORT-RANGE INTERCEPTOR TO SHOOT DOWN INCOMING ICBM WARHEADS USING NEUTRON FLUX.
THIS IS NOT A NUKE THE WAY YOU'RE THINKING, MARIPOSA. A NEUTRON BURST OVER ENEMY TERRITORY WOULD KILL THE INHABITANTS BUT LEAVE THE AREA TO BE QUICKLY REOCCUPIED ONCE THE RADIATION DISSIPATED.
STONE WANTS TO CLEAR THE LAND AND THEN MOVE IN?

LAND IS EVERYTHING TODAY. TERRITORY. THE WARLORDS ARE FIGHTING FOR POWER. THE MORE AREA A WARLORD CONTROLS THE MORE POWER HE HAS.
WHAT GOOD IS LAND IF YOU'RE GOING TO DROP A WEAPON OF MASS DESTRUCTION ON IT?
THIS IS ABOUT MORE THAN THE LAND, DARK CLOUD. CONTROL OVER MORE LAND MEANS CONTROL OVER MORE PEOPLE. IT MEANS A LARGER ARMY FOR STONE AND MORE WORKERS FOR HIS MINES. IT MEANS HE'LL BE ONE STEP CLOSER TO RULING OVER EVERYTHING THAT USED TO BE AMERICA.
I'M GOING TO MAKE SURE STONE NEVER SETS OFF THAT BOMB. I'M GOING TO STEAL IT.
MARIPOSA, PLEASE. THIS IS NOT YOUR FIGHT. I'VE HEARD RUMORS OF FREEDOM FIGHTERS. TRAINED SOLDIERS HIDING IN THE CANYONS. THIS IS THEIR FIGHT.
I KNOW YOU HAVE TAKEN IT UPON YOURSELF TO KEEP OUR HOME SAFE FROM INVADERS. BUT YOU ARE ONE GIRL AGAINST AN ARMY. KLAATU IS NOT INVINCIBLE. I CANNOT LOSE YOU, MARIPOSA.
WE CAN'T RELY ON RUMORS OF FREEDOM FIGHTERS. THERE'S NO ONE ELSE, RICARDO.
THIS IS A FIGHT YOU CAN'T WIN, DARK CLOUD. PROMISE ME YOU'LL STAY AWAY.
I... I PROMISE.
IT KILLS ME TO LIE TO HIM. BUT SOMETIMES KEEPING THINGS FROM OUR LOVED ONES IS AS MUCH FOR THEIR PROTECTION AS TAKING UP ARMS AGAINST AN ENEMY.

KLAATU AND I WAIT UNTIL RICARDO IS FAST ASLEEP TO SNEAK OUT.
WHEN RICARDO FOUND ME I WAS WEARING A LOCKET CONTAINING A PICTURE OF MY MOTHER AND HIM AS A YOUNG MAN.
HE SAYS HE KNEW MY MOTHER LONG AGO.
HE LOVED HER.
IT'S QUIET TONIGHT, BUT KEEP YOUR GUARD UP, KLAATU.
COPY.
I ALWAYS THOUGHT IT A STRANGE COINCIDENCE THAT HE WOULD FIND THE ONE PERSON IN THE WORLD WEARING A LOCKET WITH HER PICTURE IN IT.
I'M REALLY HOPING THAT MERC DIDN'T LOCK THIS ON US...
...MAYBE YOU SHOULD HAVE KILLED HIM, KLAATU.

NOT LOCKED. GLAD WE DIDN'T KILL THAT GUY.
RICARDO SAYS THERE ARE NO COINCIDENCES...

IT'S EMPTY.
I DON'T LIKE THIS.
...IT WAS MEANT TO BE.

YOU ARE SURROUNDED! COME OUT SLOWLY. FINGERS INTERLOCKED BEHIND YOUR HEADS.

KLAATU, THE HATCH. WE HAVE TO MOVE. NOW!
A TRAP. I KNEW IT WAS TOO QUIET.

IF I MAKE IT OUT OF THIS ALIVE, I'M GONNA GET ONE HELLUVA "I TOLD YOU SO" FROM RICARDO...

I KNEW SOMEONE HAD BROKEN INTO MY MUNITIONS DEPOT. I FIGURED WHOEVER IT WAS WOULD BE BACK AGAIN AT SOME POINT, I JUST DIDN'T THINK IT'D BE SO SOON. WHAT A PLEASANT SURPRISE TO NOT BE KEPT IN SUSPENSE.
I BARELY HEAR STONE'S PONTIFICATION. I'M MORE FOCUSED ON THE MERC WHO LET US GO.

SONOVABITCH SET US UP.

DEFINITELY SHOULD HAVE KILLED HIM.

AFTER YOUR LITTLE RAID ON MY WEAPONS SURPLUS, ONE OF MY SECURITY ADVISORS SHOWED ME A PECULIAR VIDEO OF THE BREAK IN AND I SAW SOMETHING I JUST HAD TO HAVE.

TURN THE ROBOT OVER TO ME. COMMAND CODES. OVERRIDE PROTOCOLS. ALL OF IT AND I'LL LET YOU WALK RIGHT OUT THE FRONT GATE. SCOUT'S HONOR.

STILL A WILD ANIMAL. I'M IMPRESSED YOU'RE STILL ALIVE. IT'S BEEN A LONG TIME. YOU WERE, OF COURSE, LESS FERAL WHEN LAST WE MET.
<TAH'U-TAK'A!>
WHEN LAST WE MET? I ASSURE YOU THIS IS THE FIRST TIME WE'VE EVER CROSSED PATHS.
YOU REALLY DON'T REMEMBER, DO YOU? CURIOUS. WHAT HAPPENED TO YOU AFTER ALL THOSE YEARS?

I'VE COME FOR THE NEUTRON BOMB. GIVE IT TO ME AND I'LL LET YOU LIVE... YOU CAN WALK RIGHT OUT THE FRONT GATE. SCOUT'S HONOR.
YOU'LL LET ME LIVE?!? HAHA! YOU'VE GOT CAJONES.
KLAATU, WASTE THIS PRICK!

BOOM!
THE ROOF BENEATH KLAATU'S FEET EXPLODES WITHOUT NOTICE.

KLAATU!!!

LIKE I SAID, I SAW SOMETHING I JUST HAD TO HAVE...

...AND WHEN I WANT SOMETHING. I TAKE IT.

YOU THINK YOU CAN STOP HIM! YOU HAVE NO IDEA THE STORM HE'S ABOUT TO UNLEASH! YOU BETTER LET ME GO!
THAT'S AN ELECTROMAGNETIC NET. IT SENDS OUT AN E.M.P. PULSE NEUTRALIZING THE MECHANICS OF THE TARGET. IT WAS DESIGNED TO STOP A TRUCK TRAVELING AT 80 MILES PER HOUR DEAD IN ITS TRACKS. I THINK I'LL BE OKAY.

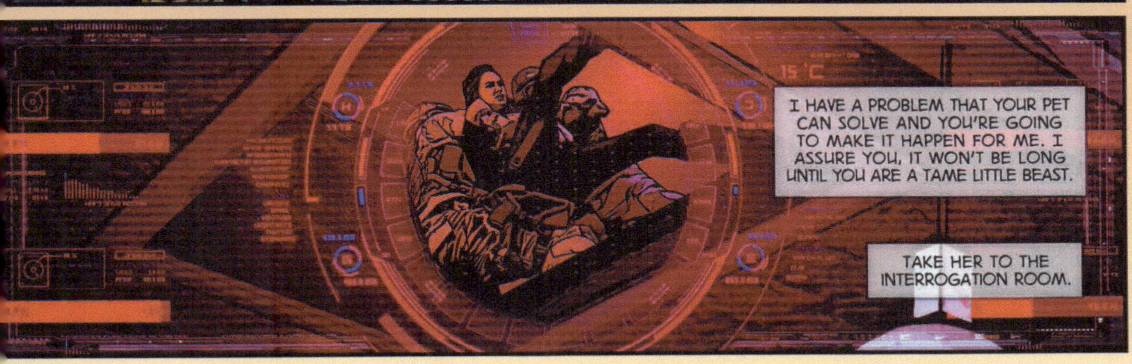

I HAVE A PROBLEM THAT YOUR PET CAN SOLVE AND YOU'RE GOING TO MAKE IT HAPPEN FOR ME. I ASSURE YOU, IT WON'T BE LONG UNTIL YOU ARE A TAME LITTLE BEAST.
TAKE HER TO THE INTERROGATION ROOM.

AAHHH!!!

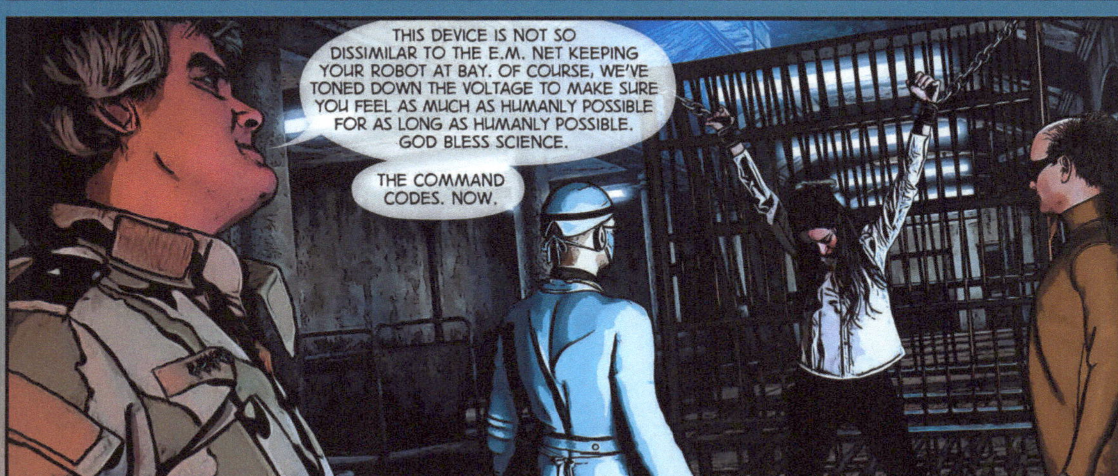

THIS DEVICE IS NOT SO DISSIMILAR TO THE E.M. NET KEEPING YOUR ROBOT AT BAY. OF COURSE, WE'VE TONED DOWN THE VOLTAGE TO MAKE SURE YOU FEEL AS MUCH AS HUMANLY POSSIBLE FOR AS LONG AS HUMANLY POSSIBLE. GOD BLESS SCIENCE.
THE COMMAND CODES. NOW.

YOU'RE GOING TO DIE STONE.
I'M HANGING ON BY A THREAD, BUT I CAN STILL MUSTER THE STRENGTH TO SPIT IN HIS FACE.

I WANT TO SAY THAT I GET NO PLEASURE IN TORTURING YOU, BUT THAT'D BE A LIE. THE TRUTH IS, I WANT YOU TO RESIST. I WANT YOU TAKE AS MUCH PAIN AS YOU CAN BEAR AND THEN I WANT YOU TO TAKE SOME MORE.
HIT HER AGAIN.

AAHHHH!!!!

GIVE ME THE COMMAND CODES!

A FEW MORE ROUNDS OF THIS AND YOU'LL BE TELLING ME EVERY DEEP DARK SECRET YOU'VE EVER KEPT...
...TAKE HER AWAY. WE'LL START AGAIN IN A FEW HOURS.

FIVE YEARS AGO.

YOU'LL BE A TAME LITTLE BEAST YET!

IT HAD BEEN A YEAR SINCE I BECAME A RUNAWAY.

AAHHH!!!

A SURVIVOR.

THREE DAYS IN THE DESERT.
...HELP ME...
NO WATER. NO FOOD.
I AM THE DESERT. THAT WHICH THEY CALL EARTH MOTHER.

TAKE MY HAND, CHILD. I TAKE ALL WHO COME TO ME AND MAKE THEM MY OWN. TAKE MY HAND AND I SHALL GIVE YOU A HOME.

AS PROOF OF OUR BOND, YOUR SENSES WILL BE ALIVE LIKE YOU HAVE ONLY DREAMED OF...
CHILD... HOW DID YOU WIND UP OUT HERE ALL ALONE?
MARIPOSA, WE MUST GET YOU HOME.
THAT LOCKET... IT'S THE ONE I GAVE TO ALICIA 20 YEARS AGO!
MI AMOR? COULD THIS BE THE DAUGHTER OF THE ONLY WOMAN WHOM I HAVE EVER LOVED... AND LOST?

THAT WASN'T A DREAM. THAT WAS SOMETHING ELSE. MY PAST. RICARDO FINDING ME IN THE DESERT.
WHY HAVEN'T I REMEMBERED THAT UNTIL NOW? THERE MUST BE A REASON.
SOMEONE'S COMING.
I DON'T KNOW IF I HAVE THE STRENGTH TO FIGHT.
I FEIGN BEING ASLEEP. MAYBE THEY WON'T TAKE ME BACK TO STONE'S TORTURE CHAMBER IF THEY THINK I'M STILL INCAPACITATED FROM THE LAST BOUT.
I WAS HOPING TO GET SOME TIME WITH YOU ALONE, LITTLE GIRL.
THERE IS NO ESCAPING THE TORTURE.

STILL UNCONSCIOUS. GOOD. I WASN'T IN THE MOOD FOR A STRUGGLE. NO REASON THIS CAN'T BE ROMANTIC.
ON SECOND THOUGHT, I'M FINDING THAT FIGHTING STRENGTH.
YOU BITCH! MY GODDAM MOUTH!
IF I CAN JUST REACH HIS BOOT KNIFE...
HOW'S THAT FOR ROMANTIC?

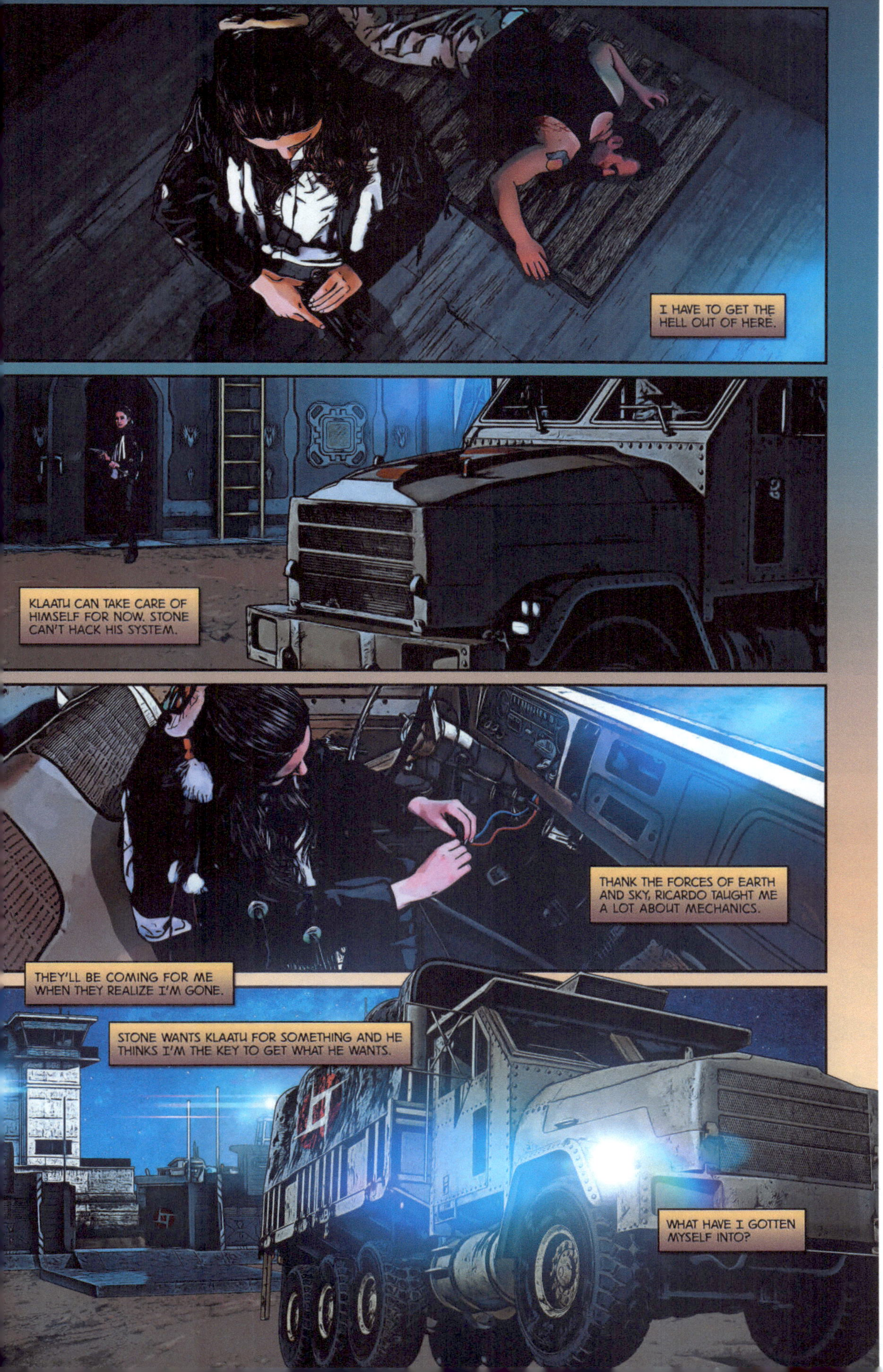

I HAVE TO GET THE HELL OUT OF HERE.
KLAATU CAN TAKE CARE OF HIMSELF FOR NOW. STONE CAN'T HACK HIS SYSTEM.

THANK THE FORCES OF EARTH AND SKY, RICARDO TAUGHT ME A LOT ABOUT MECHANICS.
THEY'LL BE COMING FOR ME WHEN THEY REALIZE I'M GONE.

STONE WANTS KLAATU FOR SOMETHING AND HE THINKS I'M THE KEY TO GET WHAT HE WANTS.
WHAT HAVE I GOTTEN MYSELF INTO?

CHAPTER 3

I'M ONLY A FEW MILES OUT FROM STONE'S COMPOUND.
I NEED TO GAIN AS MUCH DISTANCE AS I CAN BEFORE HIS HENCHMEN ARE ON TO ME.
WHY'D I STEAL THIS TRUCK INSTEAD OF SOMETHING FASTER?

COME ON! GIVE ME EVERYTHING YOU'VE GOT!

IF I CAN MAKE IT TO THE MESA I CAN HIDE UNTIL MORNING.

I HAVE TO MAKE IT.
I DON'T THINK I CAN TAKE ANOTHER ROUND OF STONE'S TORTURE.

I HIT SOMETHING IN THE TERRAIN...
...PROBABLY A ROCK, SOMETHING I DIDN'T SEE... DAMN.

I TRY AND COURSE CORRECT, BUT THE TRUCK IS TOO HEAVY.
AAHHH!!!

A DIP IN THE EARTH. IT'S ONLY A FEW FEET BUT IT FEELS LIKE FALLING OFF A CLIFF.
FOILED BY A ROCK.

WHAT NOW?
HEADLIGHTS... I WAS FOLLOWED.

CAREFUL. SHE'S NOT EXACTLY THE "LET'S TALK" TYPE.

I THINK I'LL BE OKAY--

SHE'S GONE.

YOU REALLY SHOULDN'T HAVE FOLLOWED ME.

EASY NOW. PUT THE GUN DOWN. WE'RE HERE TO HELP.
WE'RE?

I PROMISE WE'RE NOT A THREAT. NO ONE'S GOING TO HURT YOU.
YOU?! YOU SET ME UP!

I SWEAR I DID NO SUCH THING. STONE HAS A LOT OF MEN ON SECURITY AND SURVEILLANCE DETAILS.
WE WERE ACTUALLY ON OUR WAY TO SPRING YOU OUT OF STONE'S PRISON WHEN WE SAW YOU RACE THROUGH THE GATE.
IT'S TRUE.

AND WHY THE HELL WOULD I BELIEVE YOU?

I'M THE ONE THAT HELPED YOU.

AND THEN SET A TRAP FOR ME! THAT MANIAC STRAPPED ME TO A GIANT BUG ZAPPER! YOU CALL THAT HELPING?!

I PROMISE, I NEVER MEANT YOU ANY HARM. COME WITH US. LET US HELP YOU.
WE DON'T HAVE TIME FOR THIS. BY NOW STONE'S MEN KNOW YOU'RE GONE. IT'S ONLY A MATTER OF TIME BEFORE SOMEONE WHO ACTUALLY WANTS TO HURT YOU TRACKS DOWN THE TRUCK YOU STOLE AND MAKES ALL OF OUR LIVES A LOT LESS PLEASANT. WE NEED TO GO.

KEEP THE GUN. IF YOU STILL DON'T TRUST ME, YOU CAN SHOOT ME LATER. BUT RIGHT NOW, GET IN THE JEEP.

WE KNOW YOU KNOW STONE HAS A NUCLEAR WEAPON. HE'S PLANNING ON TAKING OUT THE HOOVER DAM, WE'RE JUST NOT SURE WHY.
I DON'T KNOW IF I CAN TRUST THEM, BUT IT BEATS THE ALTERNATIVE AT THE MOMENT.
BLOWING UP THE HOOVER DAM WOULD BE INSANE. IT'S TACTICALLY NONSENSICAL. WHAT'S THE POINT OF FLOODING THE AREA IF YOU'RE GONNA DROP A NUKE ON IT?
WE SEEM TO BE ON THE SAME TEAM. I'VE NEVER REALLY HAD TEAMMATES BEFORE. ALWAYS BEEN ON MY OWN.
THAT WAS GOING FINE UNTIL TODAY. I GUESS I CAN USE ALL THE HELP I CAN GET...
HE'S NOT GOING TO BLOW IT UP. THE BOMB STONE HAS IS A NEUTRON BOMB. MINIMUM BLAST RADIUS, MAXIMUM RADIATION. HE'S GOING TO CLEAR THE TERRITORY OF THE COMPETING WARLORD AND MOVE IN WHEN THE RADIATION CLEARS.
...OF COURSE, IT WOULD SEEM THEY COULD USE ALL THE HELP THEY CAN GET, TOO.
THEIR OUTPOST IS A SAFE DISTANCE FROM STONE'S COMPOUND.
HOW DO YOU KNOW ALL THAT?
RICARDO... MY... FATHER... WAS A GOVERNMENT ENGINEER IN THE OLD WORLD...
...AND HE USED TO KNOW STONE.

YOUR ROBOT--
KLAATU.
RIGHT, KLAATU... CAN HE PHYSICALLY HANDLE RADIATED MATERIAL?
YES. HE'S A PROTOTYPE ORIGINALLY DESIGNED TO WANDER A POST-NUKE BATTLEFIELD AUTONOMOUSLY.

THERE'S A LEAK IN THE WARHEAD. STRUCTURAL DAMAGE TO THE CORE'S CASING. STONE CAN'T DEPLOY THE BOMB TO ITS TARGET WITHOUT RISKING EXPOSURE.

BUT WITH KLAATU, HE CAN HAVE THE ROBOT WALK THE NUKE RIGHT WHERE HE WANTS IT TO GO.

AND NO ONE WOULD BE ABLE TO GET CLOSE ENOUGH TO THE LEAKING WARHEAD TO STOP IT.

STONE'S PLAN WON'T WORK. IT WOULD TAKE THE ORIGINAL MAKER TO CREATE A COMPLEX OVERRIDE OF KLAATU'S PROGRAMMING FOR SOMETHING LIKE THAT. HE'S ALREADY OPERATING AS MY BODYGUARD.

MARIPOSA?

DARK CLOUD?

NO...

ALERT
...MARIPOSA, WHAT HAVE YOU DONE?

WHY ARE YOU DOING THIS?
THAT'S A PRETTY NASTY GASH YOU GOT THERE.
HASN'T ANYBODY EVER HELPED YOU BEFORE?
NO, NOT THIS... THANK YOU, BY THE WAY... WHY ARE YOU FIGHTING STONE? WHY DO YOU CARE?
I WAS A MARINE BEFORE. WHEN STONE CAME TO POWER, BLADE AND I WEREN'T GIVEN MUCH OF A CHOICE TO JOIN HIS ARMY. FIGHT FOR HIM OR DIE. FIGHT OR HAVE YOUR LOVED ONES DIE.
SO YOU FOUGHT.
YEAH... AND WHAT DO YOU KNOW, MY MOTHER STILL DIED AT STONE'S HANDS. HE WORKED HER TO DEATH IN THOSE MINES.
I'M SORRY. I... I DON'T REMEMBER MY MOTHER... I DON'T REMEMBER MUCH.
I HAD NOTHING LEFT TO LOSE AFTER THAT. THAT'S WHEN I WENT AWOL AND JOINED THE RESISTANCE.
AND BLADE...?
STONE HAS HIS SISTER. HE WEARS STONE'S UNIFORM BUT HIS LOYALTIES LIE WITH US. WE'RE FIGHTING TO FREE THE PEOPLE UNDER THE CONTROL OF A TYRANT.
AND THEN WHAT? ANOTHER WARLORD COMES AND TAKES HIS PLACE? ONE WITH EVEN MORE TERRITORY? A BIGGER ARMY?
I'VE HEARD STORIES FROM OTHER TERRITORIES OF LEADERS RISING UP WHO WANT TO BUILD A BETTER SOCIETY. THEY WANT TO REBUILD INFRASTRUCTURE NOT JUST RETAKE POWER. ORGANIZE US. ALL OF US. AS EQUALS.
STORIES.
I BELIEVE THERE'S ENOUGH GOOD LEFT IN THE WORLD TO FIGHT FOR. MAYBE THEY ARE JUST STORIES. BUT MAYBE IT'S STORIES LIKE THOSE THAT WILL GIVE HOPE TO THE PEOPLE OF THIS TERRITORY AND OTHERS TO FIGHT FOR THAT GOOD TOO. TO FIGHT FOR OUR FUTURE.

I THOUGHT I RECOGNIZED YOUR HANDIWORK, DE CASTILE.
I JUST WANT MY DAUGHTER BACK, STONE.
YOUR DAUGHTER, YOU SAY? WHAT A SMALL WORLD AFTER ALL, INDEED. WELL, RICARDO, I JUST WANT YOUR COMBAT ROBOT. WHAT DO YOU SAY WE MAKE A DEAL?
IF DARK CLOUD IS SET FREE, I WILL REPROGRAM THE ROBOT TO DO AS YOU DESIRE.
I KNEW THERE WAS A WAY WE COULD HANDLE THIS AS ADULTS.
ROBOT FIRST, I'M A MAN OF MY WORD, RICARDO.
I WANT TO SEE HER.
VERY WELL, STONE. TAKE ME TO THE ROBOT.

YOU NEED TO REMOVE THE E.M. NET.
AND LET HIM SHOOT UP THE PLACE? I THINK HE'S FINE RIGHT WHERE HE IS.
I CAN'T RECONFIGURE HIS PROCESSOR AND OVERRIDE HIS COMMAND MODULES IF THERE IS AN ELECTROMAGNETIC NET INHIBITING THE CPU... I CAN'T REPROGRAM HIM IF HE CAN'T BE TURNED ON.
...
...YES. I'LL REMOVE THE E.M. NET. BUT KNOW THIS. IF I GET THE SLIGHTEST INCLINATION THAT YOU'RE GOING TO DO SOMETHING STUPID, I WILL NOT HESITATE TO PUT A BULLET IN YOUR DAUGHTER'S SKULL.
I'M SURPRISED YOU WENT ALONG SO WILLINGLY, RICARDO. I THOUGHT THIS WOULD HAVE BEEN MORE OF A FIGHT.
I KNEW DARK CLOUD'S MOTHER WELL. I LOVED HER. SHE WAS THE ONLY WOMAN I HAVE EVER TRULY LOVED.
HOW SWEET.
WHEN HER DAUGHTER CAME INTO MY LIFE I KNEW THERE WAS NOTHING I WOULDN'T DO TO KEEP HER SAFE...
SEARCHING...
BIOCHIP SCAN RESULTS: DARK CLOUD NOT ON PREMISES
CORE
...NOTHING.

KLAATU, ENGAGE!

KRAK!

NOW, RICARDO WE HAD A DEAL!

SHE ISN'T HERE, STONE. YOU HAVE NO NEGOTIATING POWER.
IF YOU DON'T TELL THAT THING TO STAND DOWN I'LL BE REINTRODUCING YOU TO YOUR DAUGHTER ONE PIECE OF HER SKULL AT A TIME.
I'M LEAVING, STONE, AND I'M TAKING MY PROPERTY WITH ME.

LIKE HELL YOU ARE!
STOP THEM!

I WANT THAT THING NEUTRALIZED!
I WANT THE ENGINEER ALIVE! HE'S GOING TO DO AS I ASK ONE WAY OR ANOTHER.

RATATAT
MIII!!!
PING
PING

PING
PING
BRRRAAA!

KLAATU...
PING
PING

NO!!! WHAT DID YOU DO!!!

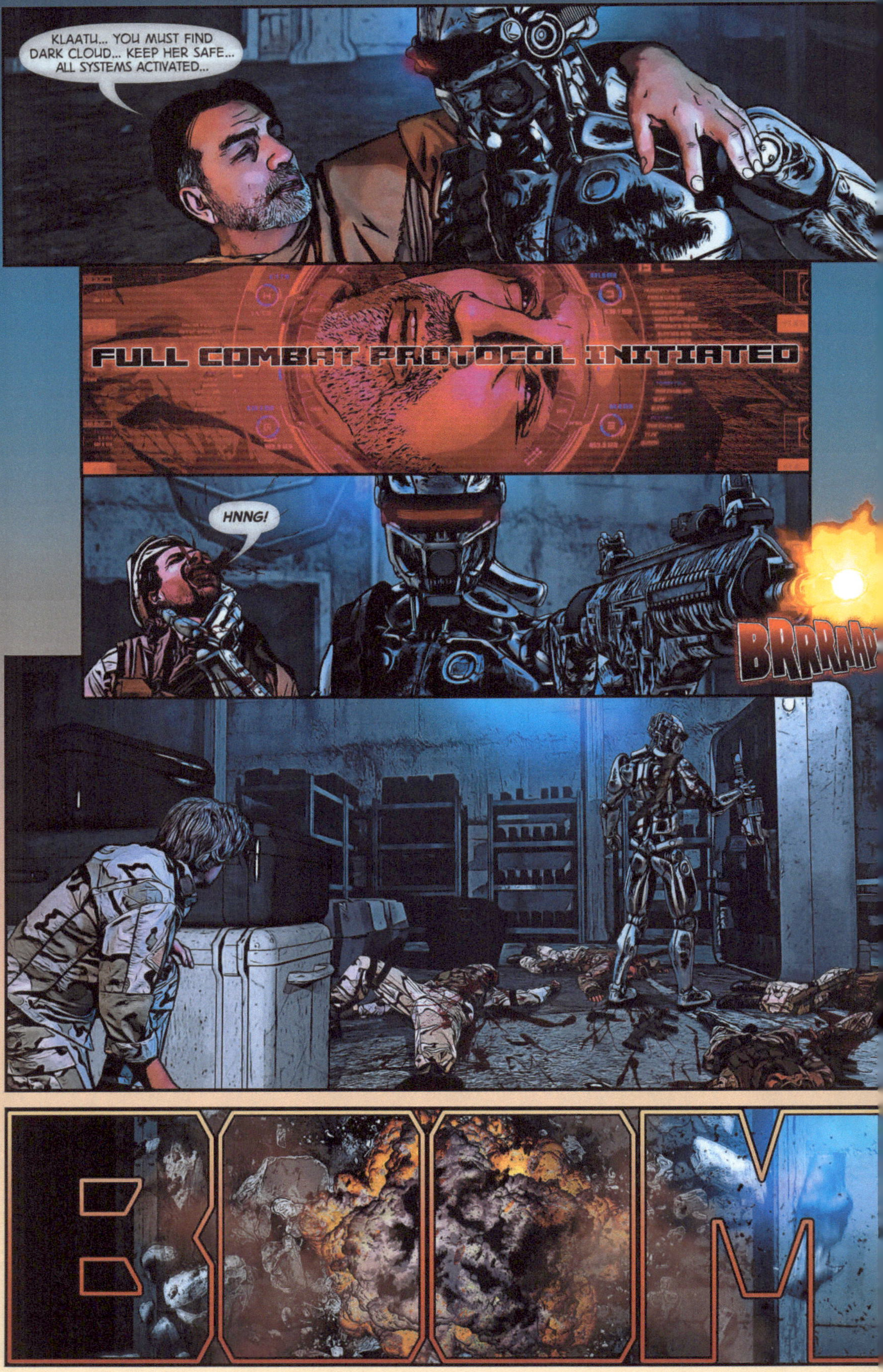

KLAATU... YOU MUST FIND DARK CLOUD... KEEP HER SAFE... ALL SYSTEMS ACTIVATED...

FULL COMBAT PROTOCOL INITIATED

HNNG!
BRRRAA

BOOM

BOOM!
AAAHHH!!!

BOOM!
HHNNG!!!

OOOGAH
OOOGAH

WHAT'S THAT?
EMERGENCY SIREN. SOMEONE'S HERE.

ALLOW ME ACCESS TO YOUR FACILITY OR I WILL MAKE MY OWN ACCESS IN 5, 4, 3...
KLAATU! HE MUST HAVE FOLLOWED MY LOCATOR CHIP!
OPEN THE GATE!

KLAATU!... I'D HUG YOU, BUT YOU'RE... DISGUSTING. WHAT HAPPENED TO YOU? HOW'D YOU GET OUT OF STONE'S COMPOUND?

THE MAKER REMOVED THE E.M. NET AND REACTIVATED ME.
RICARDO WAS AT STONE'S COMPOUND?
YES.

WELL, WHERE IS HE NOW?

ALL VITAL SIGNS WERE DISCONTINUED.

ALL VITAL SIGNS?... HE'S... HE'S DEAD?

YES.

OH GOD, NO! HE CAN'T BE DEAD! HE CAN'T BE! WHAT DID I DO?!?

LORD OF STORMS! FORCES OF EARTH AND SKY! ARE ANY OF YOU THERE?!

LORD OF STORMS! HEAR ME! PLEASE! I FEEL SO LOST! DON'T ANY OF YOU HAVE ANYTHING TO SAY TO ME?
HOW CAN THIS BE MY PATH? HOW IS THIS UNFOLDING AS IT HAS TO?
HOW CAN THIS BE MEANT TO BE?

YOU DEMAND STRENGTH AND YET I SUFFER. I NEED YOUR HELP.
ANY OF YOU... WHY WON'T YOU ANSWER ME?

OH, RICARDO,
I'M SO SORRY.

I SHOULDN'T HAVE
GONE BACK. I SHOULD
HAVE LISTENED. I SHOULD HAVE
JUST STAYED HOME AND BEEN
THE OBEDIENT DAUGHTER
YOU DESERVED.

YOU DIDN'T
DESERVE THIS.

I LOVE
YOU.

CORPORAL, YOUR PRESENCE IS BEING REQUESTED IN THE WAR ROOM.
ME?

WAR ROOM
04-10-15
DOOR 42
FRAME D-8

CORPORAL, GOOD OF YOU TO JOIN US. YOU'RE JUST IN TIME FOR THE MISSION BRIEFING.

AND YOU'RE SURE THIS INTELLIGENCE IS GOOD?
RIGHT FROM THE HORSE'S MOUTH.
IT DIDN'T SEEM ODD TO YOU THAT YOU WERE INVITED TO A MISSION BRIEFING OUT OF THE BLUE?

IT DID AT FIRST, BUT STONE WANTS HEIGHTENED SECURITY DETAIL AND SURVEILLANCE UNTIL THE MISSION IS COMPLETE. HE'S PARANOID.
IT MAKES SENSE. YOUR FRIEND OVER HERE BLEW HALF HIS OUTPOST TO KINGDOM COME.
SO STONE IS PLANNING ON SENDING A BOAT DOWN THE COLORADO RIVER TOWARD THE HOOVER DAM LOADED WITH GOODS AS A PEACE OFFERING TO THE NEIGHBORING WARLORD?

RIGHT. ONLY HE'S THROWING IN AN EXTRA TREAT, A NUCLEAR WARHEAD. THE CONVOY LEAVES TO DEPLOY THE WEAPON TOMORROW AT SUNSET. THE CONVOY WILL CHAPERONE THE BOMB UNTIL THEY ARE JUST OUTSIDE OF THE NEUTRON BLAST RADIUS AND THEN SEND IT DOWNRIVER TO BLACK CANYON.
WELL, THEN I GUESS WE HAVE TO TAKE OUT THAT CONVOY.
THE NUKE HAS TO BE PRIMED TO REACH CRITICAL MASS AND ILLICIT A NUCLEAR EXPLOSION. IT IS IMPERATIVE THAT WE GET THE BOMB BEFORE IT'S PRIMED FOR ITS FINAL LEG DOWNRIVER.
REMEMBER, WE HAVE TO BE CAREFUL AROUND THIS THING. EVEN IF IT ISN'T PRIMED, THE BOMB STILL CARRIES AN ACTIVE CONVENTIONAL EXPLOSIVE... SO TRY NOT TO SHOOT AT IT.

WHAT HAPPENS IF THE CONVENTIONAL EXPLOSIVE GOES OFF?
EFFECTIVELY, THE BOMB WILL BE NEUTRALIZED.
ISN'T THAT A GOOD THING?
NOT IF YOU'RE NEAR THE BOMB.

IF THAT'S NOT ENOUGH TO WORRY ABOUT, THE BOMB IS STILL LEAKING, SO BE CAREFUL. WE SUSPECT IT WILL BE HEAVILY INSULATED AND UNDER COVER. OUR BEST COURSE OF ACTION IS TO RECOVER THE BOMB AND NEUTRALIZE IT WHEN WE GET IT FAR ENOUGH AWAY FROM STONE.

WHAT ARE WE WAITING FOR?
GEAR UP, KLAATU. WE'VE GOT A NUCLEAR BOMB TO STEAL.

CHAPTER 4

WE TAKE POSITION ALONG THE RAVINE AND AWAIT THE CONVOY.
THESE GUYS ARE GOOD. YOU'D NEVER KNOW THERE WAS ANYONE HERE. STONE'S NOT GOING TO KNOW WHAT HIT HIM.

WHEN THE CONVOY ARRIVES, WAIT UNTIL THEY'RE DEEP ENOUGH INTO THE PASS BEFORE DEPLOYING YOUR SQUADRONS INTO POSITION. BLADE TO THE EAST. DARK CLOUD TO THE WEST.
WE'VE GONE OVER THE PLAN COUNTLESS TIMES. WE SURROUND THEM. WE KILL THEM IF WE HAVE TO. WE TAKE THE NUKE. WE RUN.
THERE ARE CAVES IN THE AREA I KNOW WHERE WE CAN HIDE WHILE NEUTRALIZING THE BOMB.

WE'RE ONLY GONNA GET ONE SHOT AT THIS. IF THEY GET PAST US HERE, THERE'S NOTHING STOPPING THEM FROM SETTING OFF THAT NUKE.
STILL... SOMETHING DOESN'T FEEL RIGHT... LIKE THIS WHOLE THING SEEMS TOO SIMPLE. NOTHING'S EVER THAT SIMPLE WITH MEN LIKE STONE.
THE ANSWER IS OBVIOUS TO ME.

KLAATU AND I ARE LEAVING.
YOU'RE WHAT?!
COME ON, KLAATU.
STONE'S NOT COMING... WE'RE IN THE WRONG PLACE.

WHAT DO YOU MEAN YOU'RE LEAVING? WE HAVE A MISSION TO CARRY OUT. WE NEED YOU.
THIS IS A RUSE. DON'T ASK ME HOW I KNOW. YOU WOULDN'T BELIEVE ME IF I TOLD YOU. STONE ISN'T COMING THROUGH THIS RAVINE AND NEITHER IS THE BOMB.

SO, WHAT, YOU'RE GONNA QUIT ON US JUST LIKE THAT? I BELIEVED IN YOU.
I'M NOT QUITTING. I'M GOING AFTER STONE AND THE BOMB. I THINK... NO... I KNOW THAT HE'S TRAVELING WEST OF HERE. I'D TRY AND TALK YOU INTO FOLLOWING ME, BUT YOU WON'T AND WE DON'T HAVE TIME TO WASTE.

AND WHAT INTEL DO YOU HAVE THAT SUPERSEDES STONE TELLING ME TO MY FACE THAT HE'S COMING THROUGH HERE?
I TOLD YOU YOU WOULDN'T BELIEVE ME. STAY HERE. CARRY OUT THE MISSION. IF I'M WRONG, YOU'LL BE ABLE TO TAKE OUT THE CONVOY JUST FINE WITHOUT ME; YOU HAVE PLENTY OF FIGHTERS HERE. IF I'M RIGHT, HIGH TALE IT WEST AND FIND ME. I'M PRETTY SURE I'LL NEED BACKUP.

ALRIGHT, LORD OF STORMS, I JUST LEFT TWO SQUADRONS OF FREEDOM FIGHTERS TO GO TAKE ON A WARLORD AND HIS ARMY ALONE...
...IF YOU'RE WAITING FOR SOMETHING, NOW'S THE TIME.

KAWWW!!! KAWWW!!!

HERE WE GO. RIGHT ON SCHEDULE.
SO MUCH FOR DARK CLOUD'S SIXTH SENSE.

WHAT THE...?

FIRE!
BOoOMM!!!
BOOOMM!!!
AAAHHH!!!
DON'T EVEN BLINK.
UMM, COYOTE JOE... WE HAVE A PROBLEM.

WHAT DO YOU MEAN A PROBLEM?
THERE'S NOTHING HERE... AND I DON'T SEE ANY PERSONNEL OTHER THAN THE DRIVERS.
WHERE'S THE NUKE? WHAT IS THIS?
CORPORAL BLADE WAS FED FALSE INTEL. GENERAL STONE KNEW THERE WAS A LEAK AND HE KNEW IT WOULD GET BACK TO YOU. WE WERE JUST A DIVERSION. IT'S TOO LATE. YOU'LL NEVER CATCH THEM.

DARK CLOUD.
SHE'S ABOUT TO TAKE ON AN ARMY BY HERSELF.

WE'RE GETTING CLOSER.
MY SENSORS DETECT NO EMPIRICAL DATA TO SUGGEST THAT WE ARE POSITIONING OURSELVES CLOSER TO GENERAL STONE'S CONVOY.
I TOLD YOU, WHAT I CAN SEE CAN'T BE DETECTED BY ANY SENSORS.

THERE. A CAMPFIRE.
THE LAST STRETCH FROM HERE TO THE RIVER IS PRETTY ROUGH TERRAIN. STONE MUST BE WAITING TILL DAYBREAK...

AFFIRMATIVE. CONFIRMING POSITIVE IDENTIFICATION OF GENERAL STONE'S ARMY.
...GUESS HE THINKS THERE'S NO WAY ANYBODY COULD FIND HIM OUT HERE.

NO BIG DEAL, WE'LL JUST STEAL A GUARDED TRUCK WITH A NUCLEAR BOMB IN IT AND RACE BACK TO REINFORCEMENTS WITH AN ENTIRE ARMY ON OUR ASS.
WE HAVE TO MAKE OUR MOVE TONIGHT. WE CAN'T FIGHT THEM ALL, BUT IF WE CAN STEAL THE TRUCK WITH THE BOMB, WE CAN RACE IT BACK TO COYOTE JOE AND THE FREEDOM FIGHTERS.
THIS COULD VERY WELL BE A SUICIDE MISSION. IF THAT'S WHAT IT TAKES TO PREVENT A NUKE FROM GOING OFF THEN THAT'S WHAT IT TAKES...
...I WON'T TELL KLAATU THAT.

OKAY, JUST LIKE WE DO WHEN WE'RE STEALING MUNITIONS.
QUIET AS A MOUSE.

THERE IT IS. IF WE CAN TAKE OUT THE GUARDS QUIETLY, WE SHOULD BE ABLE TO GET INTO THE TRANSPORT BEFORE ANYONE NOTICES.

YOU TAKE THE ONE ON THE FAR SIDE AND I'LL TAKE THE ONE ON THE NEAR. REMEMBER, QUIETLY.

...

MY REFLEXES REACT BEFORE MY BRAIN REGISTERS I'M BEING ATTACKED. WITHOUT HESITATION I THROW THE GUARD OVER MY SHOULDER.
HHNNGGG!!!

OH, SHIT!
KLAATU! NO!
THE GUNSHOT ALERTS THE CAMP THAT WE'RE HERE.
BANG!
SO MUCH FOR QUIET AS A MOUSE.
SECURE THE BOMB! GET MY WEAPON OUT OF HERE! NEUTRALIZE THE INTRUDERS! SHOOT TO KILL!
NO! KLAATU, THE TRANSPORT'S GETTING AWAY!
TING
TING
TING

KLAATU! HOLD 'EM OFF TILL I GET US ANOTHER RIDE!
RATATAT
TIME TO IMPROVISE.

COME ON!
GOTCHA!

I WILL GET THAT NUKE, STONE.
I'M NOT GONNA LET YOU SET OFF A RADIATION BOMB IN ONE OF THE LAST REMAINING PIECES OF THIS PLANET WE DIDN'T ALREADY DESTROY.

HOP ON!

WE HAVE TO CATCH THAT TRANSPORT. WE CAN'T JUST RUN IT OFF THE ROAD, STONE'S MERCS WOULD BE ON US BEFORE WE COULD UNLOAD THE BOMB AND THEN IT'S GAME OVER.
GET IN FRONT OF THE VEHICLE. I WILL TAKE IT FROM THERE.

I DON'T QUESTION HIM. IF KLAATU'S PROGRAMMING HAS A SEQUENCE CALCULATED TO ACHIEVE A SPECIFIED GOAL, IT'S USUALLY A SAFE BET TO JUST TRUST HIM.

AND BY USUALLY, I MEAN ALWAYS. AFTER ALL, HE WAS PROGRAMMED BY RICARDO.

NOT THAT HE TAKES RICARDO'S MORE TACTFUL APPROACH.

AAAGGHHH!!
AND JUST LIKE THAT, KLAATU HAS CONTROL OF THE TRANSPORT AND THE NUKE.

OKAY, MY TURN.
I GIVE THE JEEP JUST ENOUGH PRESSURE ON THE GAS TO CATCH UP TO THE TRANSPORT.
IF I TIME THIS RIGHT, I SHOULD BE ABLE TO...

...USE THE JEEP'S MOMENTUM TO CATAPULT ME ONTO THE TRANSPORT WHERE HOPEFULLY I CAN...

...GRAB ONTO THE CARGO ANCHORS AND PULL MYSELF UP.

I WASN'T COUNTING ON GUARDS INSIDE THE TRANSPORT.
HEY, YOU GUYS KNOW YOU HAVE A TAIL LIGHT OUT?
WELL, THAT OUGHTA GET THEIR ATTENTION.
WHERE'D YOU GO, GIRLIE?
THAT'S THE PROBLEM WITH MERCENARIES.
THEY DON'T HAVE THE COMBAT INTELLECT THAT REAL SOLDIERS DO.
HNGG!
RATATT
DON'T SHOOT THE NUCLEAR WARHEAD. DON'T SHOOT THE NUCLEAR WARHEAD!
STARTING TO THINK KLAATU HAD THE EASY JOB HERE.

ALRIGHT, KLAATU, SMOOTH SAILING FROM HERE. ALL WE HAVE TO DO NOW IS--
I SPOKE TOO SOON.
CRASH!
KLAATU!
WE'RE SIDESWIPED BY ONE OF STONE'S TRUCKS.
BAM!
KLAATU PULLS THE WHEEL HARD AND SLAMS HIM BACK.
THE TRUCK IS NO MATCH FOR THE TRANSPORT...
...BUT WE'RE NOT OUT OF THE WOODS YET.

RATATAT
KLAATU, I DON'T KNOW IF WE'RE GONNA BE ABLE TO KEEP THIS UP LONG ENOUGH TO GET THE BOMB BACK TO COYOTE JOE. WE CAN'T TAKE ON THE WHOLE ARMY.
DON'T SLOW DOWN! GET ME TO THAT TRANSPORT!
GENERAL, THIS IS SACRED LAND WE'RE ENTERING. IT'S HAUNTED BY EVIL SPIRITS!
IF YOU DON'T CATCH UP TO MY NUCLEAR WARHEAD, IT WON'T BE EVIL SPIRITS YOU'LL HAVE TO FEAR.
RATATAT
SCREW IT. IF THIS IS HOW I GO. THIS IS HOW I GO.
THAT BASTARD TOOK RICARDO FROM ME. HE TORTURED ME. HE THREATENED MY HOME. HE KILLED INNOCENT WOMEN AND CHILDREN.
I'M GOING TO FIGHT TO KEEP THIS WEAPON OUT OF HIS HANDS WITH EVERY LAST BREATH OF MY BEING. EVEN IF IT MEANS THAT LAST BREATH IS ON THE HORIZON.

BLAM!

IN AN INSTANT OUR CHASE COMES TO A CLOSE.
POP!

THE TIRE BLOWOUT DIPS THE FRONT OF THE TRANSPORT DOWN JUST ENOUGH TO HIT A BOULDER IN THE ROAD WE WOULD HAVE NORMALLY GONE RIGHT OVER.
BAMM!

DAMMIT.

SOMEONE GET ME MY BOMB.
LORD OF STORMS, WHERE ARE YOU? IS THIS IT?
NOT ALL AT ONCE FOR YOU. THAT'S A SMALL CALIBER ROUND. I WANT YOU TO FEEL YOUR DEATH AS RECOMPENSE FOR ALL THE AGGRAVATION YOU'VE CAUSED ME.
BANG!
I TOLD YOU I DIDN'T THINK I COULD PULL THIS OFF ALONE!
I WON'T BE DRAWN INTO YOUR LITTLE GAME. THOUGH, I SUPPOSE YOU'D HAVE TO BE A LITTLE CRAZY TO PULL THE STUNT YOU PULLED.
HOW CAN ALL THIS BE MEANT TO BE?
GENERAL, SIR, THE... THE NUKE... IT'S BEEN DAMAGED. THE CASING SECURING THE LEAK HAS BEEN RUPTURED, THE INTERNAL COMPONENTS ARE EXPOSED. WE'RE TALKING HIGH VOLATILITY, SIR.

EVERYTHING IS AS IT SHOULD BE.
NOW I CAN ACT.
DON'T YOU WORRY ABOUT THE NUKE, LITTLE GIRL. IT'LL STILL DO ITS JOB.
THE LORD OF STORMS.
HE CAME.

THE CRASH CAUSED THE CORE TO RUPTURE.
WITH VOLATILITY ALSO COMES VULNERABILITY.

THE LORD OF STORMS IS NOT ALL POWERFUL.
HE NEEDED ME TO EXPOSE THE WEAPON SO THAT HE COULD REACH IT.

KLAATU! LAVA TUBE! NOW!

HURRY!

ALL THAT IS MEANT TO BE SHALL BE.

THE ELECTROMAGNETIC DISCHARGE FROM THE LORD OF STORM'S CONCENTRATED LIGHTNING BLAST COULD ONLY HAVE REACHED THE BOMB'S CORE IF IT WERE COMPROMISED.

KRAAK!

FOR THE LAND.

FOR ITS PEOPLE.

FOR THEIR FREEDOM.

FOR RICARDO...

...AND MY MOTHER.

FOOM!
WE'RE TOO LATE!
THAT'S NOT NUCLEAR. THAT WAS THE FIRST STAGE CONVENTIONAL BLAST.
SO, SHE DID IT? SHE NEUTRALIZED THE WARHEAD?
SHE DID IT.
WHERE ARE YOU GOING?
TO FIND HER.
JOE, YOU SAW THAT BLAST.
SHE'S OKAY. SHE HAS TO BE. I HAVE TO FIND HER.

SITUATION ANALYSIS: ALL THREATS HAVE BEEN NEUTRALIZED.

I'LL SAY.

THERE ARE NO AVAILABLE VEHICLES TO MAKE OUR RETURN TO THE HOMESTEAD.
I DON'T THINK WE'RE GOING BACK HOME, KLAATU. NOT MUCH LEFT FOR ME THERE NOW. WOULDN'T BE THE SAME WITHOUT RICARDO.
WHERE TO, THEN?
I DON'T KNOW. LET'S GET OUT OF HERE, KLAATU.

RICARDO. THE MAN WHO SHOULD HAVE BEEN MY FATHER. THANK YOU... FOR EVERYTHING.
I WANT TO BELIEVE YOU WERE MORE THAN A CASUALTY OF THIS WAR.
I WANT TO BELIEVE THAT YOU, TOO, GOT A HAPPY ENDING.
I WANT TO BELIEVE THAT WHEREVER YOU ARE... YOU'RE WITH HER.

ALL THAT IS MEANT TO BE SHALL BE.
HERE BEGIN THE TALES OF DARK CLOUD...

CAST

Dark Cloud	SABRINA GOMEZ
General Stone	MARK LELAND
Blade	ALI BOXX
Coyote Joe	ERIC LUTZ
Ricardo	CHADWICK BRADBURY
Mercenaries	BRENDAN HEALY
	DAVID ABRAMSKY
Eric Stone/Freedom Fighters	JORDAN BAREL

THE LOADED BARREL STUDIOS PROCESS

By Jared Barel

If you enjoyed reading about the adventures of Dark Cloud then you might just enjoy reading about our adventures behind the scenes to bring her to life! At Loaded Barrel Studios, I developed a way to make comics that we like to call, "live-action." What we mean by live-action is that every panel of every page of each book is shot like a film with real actors playing out each scene. Those images are then illustrated to give each book the cinematic feel of reading a movie… But I'm getting way ahead of myself. There's a bit of work that needs to be done before we get that far. In the next few pages, I'm going to show you how we went from this:

To this:

STEP 1: Layout Sketches

Okay, so we've got a finished graphic novel script in our hands, now what? First things first, we need to take that script and sketch out how each panel is going to be framed and how each page is going to have those panels laid out. With this step I can start to see what the final book is going to look like. I can also see what works and what doesn't in terms of making sure the audience understands the action of the scene and can course correct anything that isn't up to par. As you'll see in Step 2, the artwork for my characters is based off of photographs. When sketching out the pages, I'm able to build performances into those characters and give my actors a better sense of what I'll need from them to bring their characters to life.

STEP 2: Photo Production

While you were reading this book you probably thought to yourself, "Damn, these characters look really real!" Well, that's because they are! Once the book is sketched out, our characters are cast and photographed against a green screen while performing each panel of the graphic novel. The actors are in full costume interacting with weapons and props to bring each panel to life. Every Loaded Barrel Studios graphic novel shoot is directed and produced just like a movie set with the only exception being that we're shooting stills instead of film. This process is what gives my work its cinematic quality... and being as I also direct movies, it kind of makes sense.

STEP 3: Photo Placement

Now that our shoot is wrapped and we have photos for every single panel in the book, the next step is to select the best take of each shot and insert those photos into our layout sketch. Now, we can start to see the page really taking shape and I can get a better sense of how the additional elements will fit in the space and how they will interact with our actors.

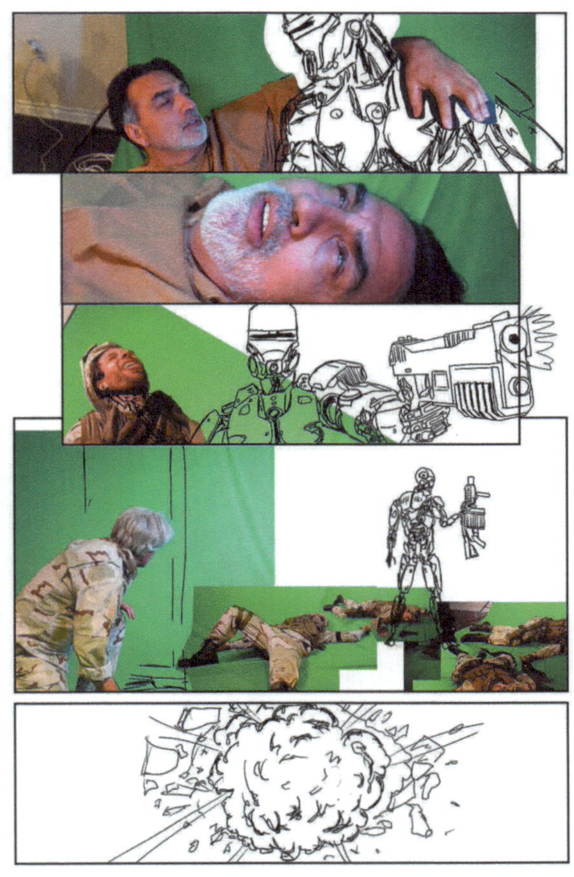

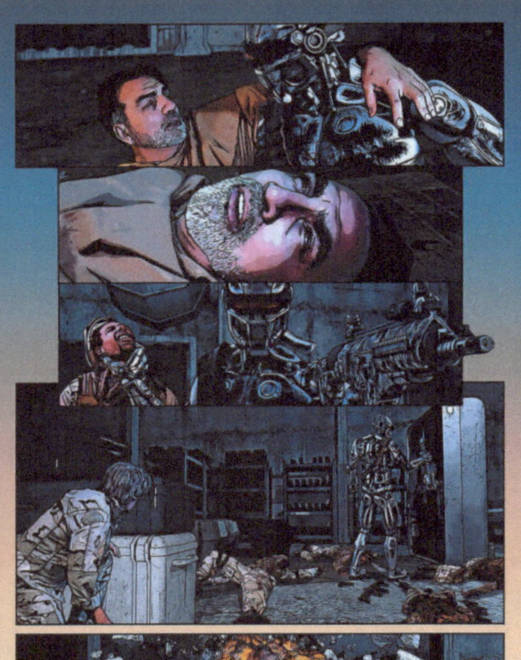

STEP 4: The Fun Part!

Now I have a bunch of photos of strangely dressed people against green backgrounds... how does that become a graphic novel? Well, if you notice our sketch has a lot of elements on each panel that we didn't necessarily shoot live -- the robot was completely uncooperative on set! Since the real Klaatu was being a jerk and since this story required a lot of unique locations and vehicles, I decided to populate many of those elements in the book with 3D models. The 3D elements allowed me to collage real and generated images in a way that maintained that lifelike, cinematic quality while still having complete control over each object in each panel. Those 3D elements along with the photographed elements (our actors) are then illustrated through a combination of photo-manipulation and traditional and digital illustration techniques.

STEP 5: Lettering and Final polish

While the above image looks pretty finished, it's still got a little ways to go before it's print ready. Lighting effects, dust and smoke, muzzle flashes, glass reflections, blood splatter, logos, and any other eye candy that can enhance each panel come together to help make the page really pop and bring our scene to life. Once all of those details are sprinkled on, the last step is to add the dialog and FX lettering and, voila, you've got yourself a finished "live-action" graphic novel page!

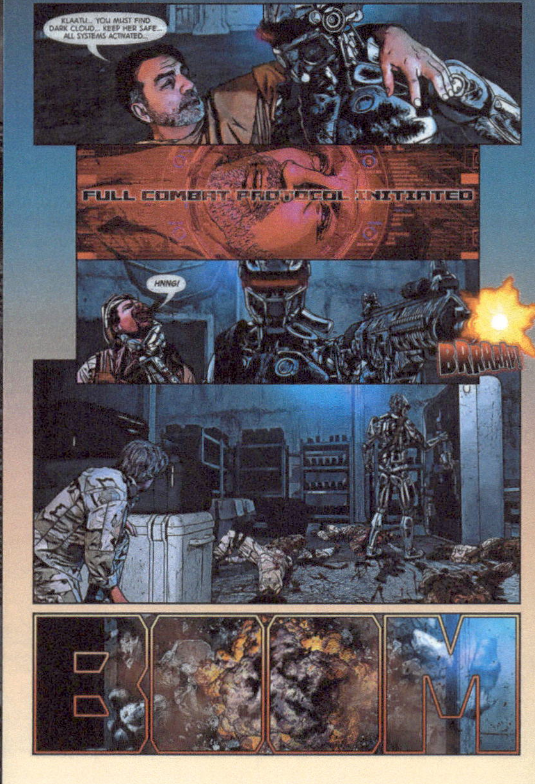

CREATOR PROFILES

SANDRA WOLFF

Sandra Wolff writes from what she knows. Although she hasn't been on a horse since her teens, and her goals require her to live in a city, rural Western skills are still a part of her make up with an emphasis on the style found in the South Western U.S. Knapping stone tools, handling a fire-arm, harvesting natural resources to make rope, shelter, and Native American style ceramics, along with many other skills and creative crafts handy in an open environment are all part of her knowledge base. She also made or customized the various parts of Dark Cloud's costume along with those of some of the other characters.

For DARK CLOUD, Sandra shared with Jared the screenplay, other files that included back-stories, character profiles and context, plus spent time going over it all with him to make sure there was a solid story, with all the nuances still intact, before panel 1 was ever designed. She knew that the script still needed something when she approached Jared. It wasn't until production began that she found out what had been missing in her self-taught education for this business was dialogue-specific. Thankfully, Jared had that covered, and with her blessing wrote the Graphic Novel adaptation.

JARED BAREL

Jared is the artist and designer behind Loaded Barrel Studios. He is the artist and writer (along with his brother, Jordan Barel) behind the award winning graphic novels BRIELLE AND THE HORROR and GREY. His other comic work includes illustrating the legendary Steve McQueen for the graphic novel series by Garbo Studios and CBS Broadcasting, STEVE MCQUEEN IN LE MANS and AND STEVE MCQUEEN CREATED LEMANS. He is also the artist for the ComicMix graphic novel release, HA.I.LEY, written by Shane Riches and produced by Paper Movies.

In addition to his comic work, Jared is also an accomplished filmmaker having directed, produced and edited the multiple award winning rock 'n roll comedy feature film, THE INCOHERENTS, distributed by Gravitas Ventures and produced by Loaded Barrel Studios. His film, illustration, and animation work has led him to work on the feature films UNCAGED and GREATLAND, with music industry clients such as Hayley Kiyoko, DMC, Starley, and Bob Moses, and corporate clients like Sprint, Anheuser-Busch, Adobe, and more.

For Jared, it was an absolute pleasure working with Sandra to bring her story to life and he looks forward to working on the sequel!

www.DarkCloudOnline.com

Want More Dark Cloud?

Go to the website www.DarkCloudOnline.com for the latest news and information, and sign up for the mailing list to be the first to hear more!

About creating the Dark Cloud website, Sandra Wolff has this to say:

"This is the birth of something. Dark Cloud is more than just a graphic novel, it's a world with a large expanse that will one day grace the silver screen. I've put it all in one place on the Dark Cloud website. Be the first to hear about Dark Cloud developments, news about the Dark Cloud movie, my general observations about different elements I incorporate in the story telling and more exclusive content. Check it all out and follow along as I work on growing all this into it's own wave. You'll be getting in on the ground floor!"

Do you like Dark Cloud? If the answer is "Yes," then go to the website for more... And tell your friends!

www.ingramcontent.com/pod-product-compliance
Lightning Source LLC
Chambersburg PA
CBHW042138120726

47911CB00022B/114